Geronimo Stilton

THE WIZARD'S WAND

THE NINTH ADVENTURE IN THE KINGDOM OF FANTASY

Scholastic Inc.

Library of Congress Cataloging-in-Publication Number: 2016007963

ISBN 978-1-338-03291-8

Text by Geronimo Stilton
Original title *Nono Viaggio nel Regno della Fantasia*
Cover by Silvia Bigolin (design) and Christian Aliprandi (color)
Illustrations by Silvia Bigolin, Carla De Bernardi, Alessandro Muscillo, Federico Brusco, Silvia Fusetti, and Piemme's Archives. Color by Christian Aliprandi.
Graphics by Marta Lorini, Chiara Cebraro, Michela Battaglin, and Daria Colombo.

Special thanks to AnnMarie Anderson
Translated by Julia Heim
Interior design by Kay Petronio

10 9 8 7 6 5 4 3 2 1   16 17 18 19 20

Printed in Malaysia   108

First edition, September 2016

Protectors of the Kingdom of Fantasy

Geronimo Stilton

I am a bestselling author and publisher of *The Rodent's Gazette*, the most famouse newspaper on Mouse Island. This is my ninth trip to the Kingdom of Fantasy.

Scribblehopper

I'm a literary frog and I dream of someday writing a book! I am Geronimo's official guide on his visits to the Kingdom of Fantasy.

Blossom

I am the Queen of the Fairies. Some call me the White Queen or the Lady of Peace and Happiness. I hope to unite the world in love, light, and harmony.

Blue Rider

I am a brave, daring, and courageous knight. They call me Defender of the Weak, and Hero to the Helpless and Hopeless!

Chatterclaws

I am a chatty, opinionated hermit crab. I am the messenger for Her Royal Majesty, Queen Blossom.

Invisible Cloak

I was created by seven generations of spiders, but no one has ever seen me! I am completely invisible.

Cleverwing

I am the slyest raven in the Kingdom of Fantasy and a cleverness expert. You can find pretty much anything in my treasure chest.

IT ALL STARTED LIKE THIS . . .

My dear mouse friends,
you know who I am, right?

My name is Stilton, *Geronimo Stilton*, and I run *The Rodent's Gazette*, the most famouse newspaper on Mouse Island!

I'm about to tell you the story of another one of my magical journeys to the *Kingdom of Fantasy* . . .

Dear mouse friends . . .

Yes, I'm talking about the **most beautiful place in the world**, the home of fairies, gnomes, giants, elves, pixies, dragons, unicorns, and mythical talking animals!

It all started exactly like this . . .

It was March 20, the first day of **Spring**. That morning I was supposed to attend a conference in **CHEDDARVILLE**. I had to wake up super early to get to the airport in time for my flight. So I set my **ALARM CLOCK** . . . but it didn't work! Instead of being super early, I woke up **super late**!

CHEDDARVILLE BOOK FAIR

March 20
Fantasy Literature
Conference
10:00 a.m.

Featuring guest speaker
Geronimo Stilton!

It's so late!

My alarm clock didn't work!

I jumped in the shower, but the water was **freezing** —

the hot-water heater was broken!

I got dressed quickly and left in a hurry, but a button got caught on the doorknob and my jacket **ripped**!

So I went back inside to change. At that point, I was extremely late!

I finally got outside and looked for a taxi, but of course I couldn't find one!

Luckily, I arrived at the airport just in time to board the plane. But the flight was **terrible**. I suffered from airsickness the whole time!

I took a freezing shower . . .

I caught my button on the doorknob and ripped my jacket . . .

and the flight was terrible!

The conference was canceled . . .

I had lost my keys . . .

and the house had flooded!

I arrived just in time for the start of the conference, only to discover that it had been canceled at the last minute with no notice!

I returned home, only to discover I had lost my house keys and was now locked out!

When the locksmith finally let me in, I discovered that the house was flooded because I had left the shower running that morning!

I went straight to bed. But I was so tired I

couldn't fall asleep.

So I turned on my **computer** to write a new chapter of my latest book. But I accidentally pressed the **wrong** button and erased everything!

Nooooo!

I deleted the whole book!

"Noooo!" I squeaked. "Why me?!"

What a horrible day!

I **SIGHED**. How I wished I were in the *Kingdom of Fantasy*! There, I could use my **imagination** to fix any problem.

What a day!

I finally went to bed, exhausted . . .

I finally fell into a restless sleep, full of strange **dreams**

At midnight I woke up suddenly because I heard bells *jingling*. I ran to the window. Outside, I saw a **SILVER CARRIAGE** being pulled through the air by **THIRTEEN SILVER UNICORNS**.

ABOARD THE SILVER CARRIAGE

I **BLINKED**. Wait, what? Were those really UNICORNS? And was that carriage really *flying* through the air by my house?!

A frog poked his head out the driver's seat.

"Knight!" he **SHOUTED**. "Are you ready for a new adventure? Come on! We *leave* immediately!"

I shook my snout, still GROGGY from sleep. Had the cheese slipped off my cracker?

The frog hopped out of the carriage and jumped onto my windowsill. It was my friend **SCRIBBLEHOPPER**! He's a literary frog, an aspiring author, and my official guide when I visit the *Kingdom of Fantasy*.

"Come on, Knight!" he said again, more **URGENTLY**. "Climb aboard. We're leaving!"

"Um, but I need to pack my bag," I replied.

Scribblehopper
A first-class literary frog, he graduated from the prestigious Elvish University with a degree in mythology, fableology, and comparative legendology. He is also an expert in witchery, sirenology, dragonology, pixieology, gnomeology, giantology, and fairyology. He is Geronimo's official guide to the Kingdom of Fantasy.

"I'm not ready to go on a trip. It's the middle of the **NIGHT**!"

"That's no excuse, Knight!" Scribblehopper croaked impatiently. "There's a real **EMERGENCY** in the Kingdom of Fantasy. Why else would I have come to find you? Sheesh! Come on, our queen is **MISSING**!"

We're leaving!

"*Blossom* is missing?!" I shouted. "Why didn't you say so? I'll be right there!"

I quickly got dressed and jumped aboard the silver carriage, which was *HOVERING* right next to my window.

"Welcome aboard, Knight," Scribblehopper said. "I have the honor of being the captain of —"

Before he could finish, the unicorns **DARTED** forward and took off.

MOLDY MOZZARELLA! Airplanes were bad, but that carriage was so much worse. I thought I might toss my cheese!

As we raced through the air, Scribblehopper called out:

"ON THE WINGS OF THE WIND
THE SILVER CARRIAGE WILL FLY,
TO THE KINGDOM OF FANTASY
THROUGH THE STARRY NIGHT SKY!"

Well, I guess some things never change. My friend's poetry was still PRETTY AWFUL!

The
Kingdom
of
Fantasy

WHAT A FRIGHT . . .
I MEAN FLIGHT!

Scribblehopper pointed to a chameleon wearing an *elegant* blue uniform.

"This is **PRISM**, our flight attendant," Scribblehopper said. "She also happens to be the cousin of Boils the chameleon."

Prism, the flight attendant

Of course! I knew she looked *familiar*. I had met Boils on some of my previous trips to the Kingdom of Fantasy.

Next, Scribblehopper introduced me to a 𝔰mall bat carrying a guitar.

"And this is **Batty Matty**,"

Batty Matty

he explained. "He will entertain us during our journey by singing and playing his guitar."

"Knight! Fasten your seat belt immediately," Prism yelled at me. "And please remain seated during the duration of the flight. Thank you!"

"Don't worry, I wouldn't even think about moving," I replied, my whiskers trembling in fright as the Silver Carriage veered to the RIGHT and then to the LEFT, diving downward and then soaring upward.

Holey cheese! I felt so sick.

"Faster, Blossom's faithful subjects!" Scribblehopper shouted into the wind.

Spurred on by his words, the unicorns galloped faster and faster. As the carriage BOUNCED up and down, Prism wouldn't stop chattering in my ear.

"Would you like a beverage, sir? Or maybe a slice of cheese?"

Ugh! The thought of food made me feel **one hundred times worse**!

"Captain Scribblehopper is such a good pilot," Prism continued. "I don't think he'll **crash**, do you?"

The carriage dipped suddenly.

"Or maybe he will!" Prism added.

Then Batty Matty began to *strum* his guitar and sing:

"We fly through the sky but don't know why,
The carriage swoops low and then goes high.
No one knows if we might crash,
And fall to the ground with a great big smash!"

"Please stop," I squeaked to the bat. "You might distract the pilot!"

"I'm not worried," he replied with a shrug. "If we crash, I have wings. Worst case, I'll FLY!"

"We're prepared for anything, Knight," Prism added. Then she showed me a small parachute she wore under her uniform. "I never, ever take it off, just in case."

Cheese niblets! Where was MY parachute? I was about to ask, when the carriage began to vibrate violently.

"Turbuleeeeeeence!" Scribblehopper shouted. "Fasten your seat belts, everyone!"

Finally, after a very long night of traveling, a golden sphere appeared on the horizon. It was dawn and I was still alive! Squeak!

"We are approaching CRYSTAL CASTLE," Scribblehopper ANNOUNCED. "We will land in approximately twenty minutes.

Did you fasten your seat belt?

Crew, prepare for arrival!"

"Fasten your seat belt, Knight!" Prism yelled. "Come on, hurry up!"

"B-but I —" I stuttered, trying to explain that I had never **unbuckled** my belt.

"No time to argue," Prism cut me off. "Just do it quickly! And put your tray table back up. **DO IT, KNIGHT!**"

At that moment, the carriage lurched into a **NOSEDIVE**.

"Ahhhhhh!" I squeaked. "Help! I don't want to crash! **I'm too fond of my fuuuuuuur!**"

A second later, we landed with an enormouse **bump**.

Even though I was wearing my seat belt, I tumbled **UPSIDE DOWN**.

Enough already!

"Hooray!" Scribblehopper shouted with joy. "I did it! We're still alive!"

Prism patted him on the back.

"My compliments on the landing!" she said. "No one would know that you learned to fly only **yesterday**!"

"Wh-what?" I said weakly. Had I heard that correctly? "You learned to fly **yesterday**?"

He nodded with satisfaction.

"Yup," he replied. "I was good, right?"

I turned as pale as a slice of mozzarella.

What a way to start my adventure!

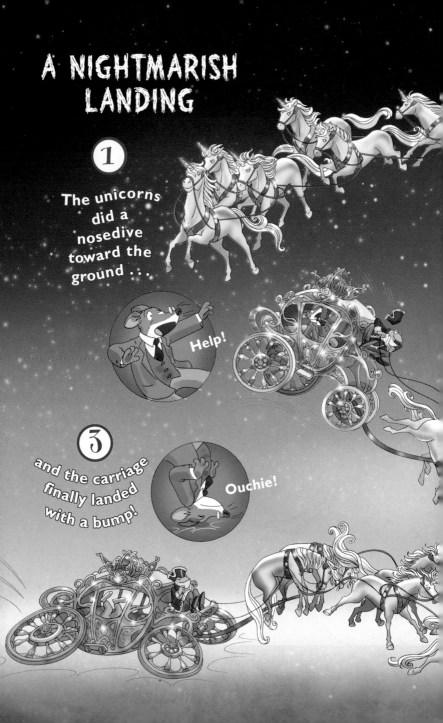

2

They turned
suddenly . . .

CRYSTAL CASTLE

A crowd of fantastical creatures immediately surrounded the silver carriage.

"It's the knight!" they murmured. "Sir Geronimo of Stilton has arrived to save our queen . . . and the *Kingdom of Fantasy*!"

The carriage door opened and a **snout** — I mean a **SHELL** — I knew appeared. It was

The knight has arrived!

Oh!

Ugh!

Hey, Sir Whatsit!

Welcome!

Huh?

my hermit crab friend Chatterclaws! I met him during my seventh trip to the Kingdom of Fantasy.

"Hey, SIR WHATSIT!" he called. "What took you so long? We've been WAITING for you to arrive for hours. Now hurry up, What's-your-name! Get down from that thingamajig!"

I shook my friend's **CLAW** and followed him inside the castle.

"Hi there, Chatterclaws," I said. "I've missed you! How is everything in the Kingdom of Fantasy?"

He shook his head.

"Ah, What's-your-name — I mean, Knight," he began. "It's not good! In fact, it's really **AWFUL**. I mean, it's just the **worst**!"

Then he began to **SOB**.

The queen has disappeared!

What?!

"Please don't cry!" I told the crab. "Just tell me what's going on so I can **HELP**!"

"A terrible thingamajig has happened," he continued. "It's really awful, and so **SCARY**! The queen has disappeared!"

I sighed, my whiskers **shaking**.

"I'd heard that," I explained. "Scribblehopper told me that. But **HOW** did it happen? **WHO** is responsible? **Where** will we find her?"

LUCKILY, someone else stepped forward. It was my friend **Blue Rider**.

"Good to see you again, Sir Geronimo," he greeted me. "I'm afraid we don't know where Blossom is, or who is **RESPONSIBLE**. And there's more: One of the

Blue Rider
A brave knight Geronimo met on his sixth journey to the Kingdom of Fantasy.

most **powerful** objects in the Kingdom of Fantasy has also disappeared!"

"What?!" I squeaked. This was worse than that time I thought everyone forgot my birthday!

The First Magical Object

The Book of a Thousand Spells

"It's true," Blue Rider replied gravely. "The Book of a Thousand Spells is gone! If it falls into the wrong hands, it could become a **terrible weapon**."

He lowered his voice. "The book contains all the **magical spells** in the Kingdom of Fantasy," he explained. "That's why all the magicians and witches want it. Do you know the **HISTORY** of the Kingdom of Fantasy, Knight?"

I shook my snout.

"Well, I'll tell you," Chatterclaws volunteered.

"Many, many years ago, Whoosy Whatsy used some thingamajigs to build a great, big whatchamacallit."

Blue Rider cleared his throat.

"Um, excuse me, Chatterclaws, but maybe it's best if I **exPLaiN**," he offered gallantly. "Many, many moons ago, King Regal III built Crystal Castle, the heart of the Kingdom of Fantasy. He did this using three extremely **POWERFUL** magical objects:

1. The Book of a Thousand Spells

2. The Crystal Sphere

3. The Whispering Wand

"The job was **ENORMOUSE**! In fact, it took **330,000 years**. The Crystalline Gnomes helped the king by bringing him precious, pure crystals from Crystal County. These crystals are what make the castle sparkle so brightly."

Building Crystal Castle

1. *THE BOOK OF A THOUSAND SPELLS*
2. THE WHISPERING WAND
3. THE CRYSTAL SPHERE
4. CRYSTALLINE GNOMES
5. CRYSTALS FROM CRYSTAL COUNTY (THE PUREST CRYSTALS IN THE ENTIRE KINGDOM OF FANTASY!)

THIS ISN'T JUST BAD . . . IT'S REALLY, REALLY BAD!

When he had finished telling the story, Blue Rider *sighed* deeply.

"Do you understand why the situation is so serious, Knight?" he asked. "Just as these three items were used to build Crystal Castle, they could be used to **DESTROY** it if they fall into the wrong hands!"

Suddenly, the door burst open. An ELFIN MESSENGER dashed in. His hat was on backward, he was panting from running so fast, and the soles of his shoes were worn out.

"I . . . **GASP** . . . must . . . give . . . **GASP** . . . you . . . **GASP** . . . some news . . ."

Then he fainted from exertion.

Chatterclaws threw a bucket of **stinky, dirty** water in his face.

"Hey, yoo-hoo!" the hermit crab shouted. "Wake up! We need to hear your **message**!"

The elf spluttered as he came to.

"I come from the faraway **EMPIRE OF THE RUBY DRAGONS**," he said softly. Then he fainted again.

This time Chatterclaws woke him by **pinching** his nose.

"Helloooooooo!" he shouted. "Come on now, wake up! We need to know what's going on, **IMMEDIATELY**!"

The elf woke again with a start.

"Th-the C-Crystal Sphere has been **STOLEN**!"

Then he fainted again. This time Chatterclaws left him alone because

Yoo-hoo! Wake up! Ouchie!

The Second Magical Object

The Crystal
Sphere

he was too **BUSY** wringing his claws with worry.

"This isn't just bad . . . it's really, really bad!" Chatterclaws moaned.

Blue Rider had turned pale.

"The CRYSTAL SPHERE is the SECOND most powerful object in the Kingdom of Fantasy," he explained solemnly. "The sphere makes it possible to **SEE** everything that happens in the kingdom while remaining unseen."

At that moment, a stork flew in through the window and collapsed on the ground in an exhausted heap.

Phew!

"Hello!" the stork whispered. "It's me, Prettyfeathers, Queen of the Pink Storks. I have awful news. The Whispering Wand has been **STOLEN!**"

This **time** it was Chatterclaws's turn to faint!

KA-BOOM!

He landed on the ground with a thud.

Two hermit crab nurses came to help. First, they gently placed him on a stretcher made of **algae**. Next, they put a **seaweed**

1 The hermit crab nurses arrived with a stretcher . . .

2 they made a cold seaweed compress . . .

3 and then they gave him a plankton shot!

compress on his forehead. Finally, they gave him a shot of concentrated **PLANKTON**.

Chatterclaws woke with a start.

"What was that?" he yelled. "It really, really **PINCHED**!"

He **LOOKED** down at the stretcher.

The Third Magical Object

"**Help!**" he shouted. "What's **wrong** with me? Am I going to **die**?"

After we had assured Chatterclaws that he was going to be just fine, Blue Rider told us more about the **WHISPERING WAND**.

The Whispering Wand

"It's the third most powerful object in the Kingdom of Fantasy!" he explained. "The creature who possesses it can use it to cast any kind of spell — **good** or **EVIL**!"

Then he lowered his voice.

"Knight, I must tell you a **SECRET**," he whispered. "But you can't tell a soul."

I placed a paw over my heart.

"The secrets of the Kingdom of Fantasy are safe with me!" I squeaked. "Rodent's honor!"

"If someone possesses all three objects — *The Book of a Thousand Spells*, the Crystal Sphere, and the Wizard's Wand — we're in **big trouble**," Blue Rider said. "If the three items are used at the same time, they could make Crystal Castle DISAPPEAR into thin air. Poof!"

"Salty seaweed!" Chatterclaws yelled. "This isn't just bad, it's REALLY, REALLY BAD!"

POOF!

The Biggest Secret in the Kingdom . . .

The three most powerful objects in the Kingdom of Fantasy are *The Book of a Thousand Spells*, the Crystal Sphere, and the Whispering Wand.

The Book of a Thousand Spells

KEEPER: Blossom, Queen of the Fairies

REGION: Kingdom of Fairies

POWER: It contains all the magical spells in the Kingdom of Fantasy.

DANGER: In the hands of the wrong creature, it could become a terrible weapon!

The Crystal Sphere

KEEPER: King Firetail

REGION: The Empire of the Ruby Dragons

POWER: Makes it possible to see everything that happens in the kingdom while remaining unseen.

DANGER: It could reveal secrets for the wrong reasons!

The Whispering Wand

KEEPER: The Two Slithering Kings

REGION: The Kingdom of the Hissing Serpents

POWER: It can perform any spell.

DANGER: In the hands of the wrong creature, it could be very destructive!

When used together, the three objects could make Crystal Castle disappear!

+ + = POOF!

WHO STOLE THE MAGICAL OBJECTS? HOW DID THEY DO IT? AND, MOST IMPORTANT, WHY?

THE QUEEN'S SECRET QUARTERS

Blue Rider gestured for me to follow him.

"Come on, Knight," he said. "I'll show you the queen's secret quarters. We may find a CLUE there."

He led me down a LONG corridor I had never been down before. First we entered Blossom's sleeping quarters. The canopy bed had drapes made of delicate silk and lace made by fairy weavers. Then we saw the bathroom. It had a CRYSTAL bathtub and shelves and shelves of sparkling bottles of perfume. Blossom's closet was full of **beautiful clothes**, each outfit more splendid than the last. And the smell of Blossom's **sweet** rose perfume was everywhere!

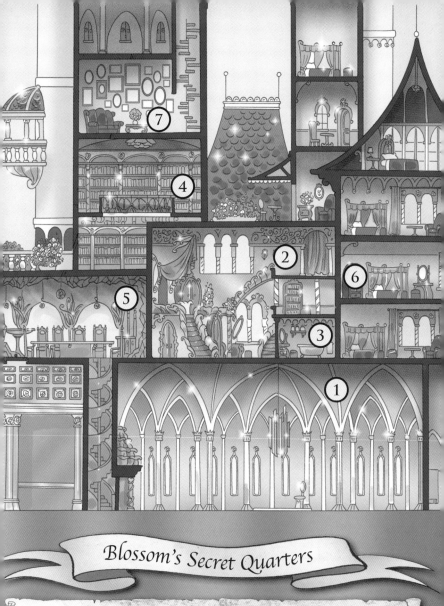

Blossom's Secret Quarters

1. THE THRONE ROOM
2. SLEEPING QUARTERS
3. BATHROOM
4. BLOSSOM'S SECRET STUDY
5. THE EMERALD CHAMBER
6. FAIRY ADVISORS' ROOM
7. THE ROOM OF MIRRORS

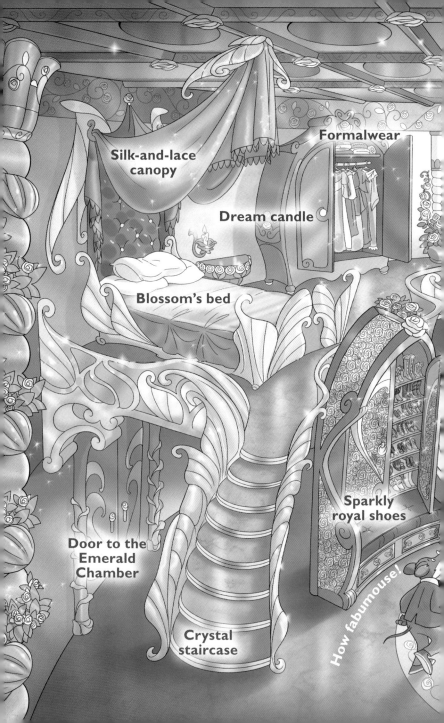

Silk-and-lace canopy

Formalwear

Dream candle

Blossom's bed

Sparkly royal shoes

Door to the Emerald Chamber

Crystal staircase

How fabumouse!

Blossom's Sleeping Quarters

Fairy mirror

Secret study

Blossom's bathroom

Her royal shoes were made of the purest sparkly crystal, and a miniature DRAGON guarded her chest of royal jewels. He glared at me and bared his teeth to let me know he was doing his job.

It was so sad seeing all of Blossom's things and not having any idea where she was!

"What can I do to help?" I asked Blue Rider. "We need to find Blossom as QUICKLY as possible!"

"Let's look for some clues," Blue Rider said as he opened the door to Blossom's secret study. "This is where Blossom keeps the fairies' secret books."

He pointed to the silver lectern in the middle of the room.

"Here's where The Book of a Thousand Spells was before it disappeared along with our queen!"

Blossom has two pairs of shoes that are identical. Can you find them?

Did this buckle come from one of Blossom's shoes?

THE SOLUTION IS ON PAGE 311.

I approached the lectern to get a better look, and I noticed a strange gold buckle on the floor.

It was a buckle from a shoe!

I picked it up and looked at it carefully. Then I went over to check Blossom's closet. Had this buckle come from one of Blossom's shoes?

FIRST CLUE

The strange gold buckle

Her closet was full of shoes of all kinds. Some of them had bows and ribbons, while others had buckles and PRECIOUS STONES. But none of the shoes were missing a gold buckle. That meant the buckle probably came off the thief's shoe!

I HAD FOUND THE FIRST CLUE . . .

THE EMERALD CHAMBER

As I thought about our first clue, Blue Rider grew even more serious.

"Knight, it's time for me to take you to one of the most *secret* places in the *Kingdom of Fantasy*," he whispered.

Chatterclaws poked his head out of a bucket full of **ALGAE**.

Wait!

"Wait!" he protested. "You can't take him there. That place has been a secret *forever and ever*!"

Honestly, I was a little offended that Chatterclaws thought I couldn't keep a *secret*. After all, my name wasn't Chatterclaws!

But Blue Rider stood up for me.

"I'm sorry, Chatterclaws, but we need Sir Geronimo's help," Blue Rider said. "He is an HONORABLE rodent. He will keep our secret."

Then Blue Rider turned toward me decisively. "Follow me," he said. "We need to *HURRY*!"

He led me to the Throne Room, where he stopped in front of a CRYSTAL FIREPLACE on the western wall. Above the fireplace was an emblem that had writing in the Fantasian alphabet etched in the center. Can you translate it?*

* You can find the Fantasian Alphabet on page 310.

It said, "Find a secret space inside this magic place." How intriguing!

Blue Rider looked around to make sure no one was spying on us. Then he pressed his hand against a **GREEN** stone beneath the writing. The back of the fireplace opened up to reveal a **secret passage**!

I followed Blue Rider inside. We climbed a winding *spiral staircase* and then went through a trapdoor in the ceiling. We emerged inside a wonderfully strange room.

Blue Rider said.

THE COUNCIL OF THE THIRTEEN SAGES

The room looked as though it had been cut from an enormouse *emerald*. The magnificent green walls sparkled and glowed, and a **great round table** sat in the center of the room. Thirteen seats **ENCRUSTED** with emeralds surrounded the table. Ten of the seats were occupied, but three remained empty.

One of the three had a rose carved in it. I could tell right away that it was *Queen Blossom's* chair!

Another empty chair had **Blue Rider's** name on it.

And the third vacant seat had **my** name on it!

Blue Rider placed a crown with SILVER leaves on my head. Then he made me slip into a SILVER toga and SILVER sandals.

THE COUNCIL OF THE THIRTEEN SAGES

According to legend, Queen Blossom relies on a council of **thirteen sages** who offer her advice and support. Their names are a secret so that no one can influence their decisions. They gather in the **Emerald Chamber**, which is hidden in a secret part of **Crystal Castle**.

The room is called the **Emerald Chamber** because it is green, shiny, and cut from an emerald. In the Kingdom of Fantasy, green is a symbol of **pure love**, and the thirteen sages gather there because of their pure love for the Kingdom of Fantasy!

Each of the sages receives an **emerald ring** and a **chair** with his or her name **carved** on it. In exchange, each sage promises to defend the kingdom.

During council meetings, the sages wear **leaf crowns** made of pure silver. Their **togas**, **sandals**, and **scepters** are also silver so they remember to keep their hearts and minds as pure as fairy silver.

Silver leaf crown

CORALINE

EMERALD

LAKENESS

STRONGHEART

BITSY
LUCKYBUG

CHATTERCLAWS

Finally, Blue Rider handed me a SILVER scepter.

I sat down at the table, feeling honored to be included in this gathering of amazing advisors.

Scribblehopper was already seated at a desk next to the table.

"Knight!" he croaked impatiently. "It's about time you arrived. We've been waiting for you!"

Then he began to solemnly list the names of everyone present and their titles within the council. I knew all those seated around the table from my previous journeys to the Kingdom of Fantasy. EVERYONE in the council was present — well, everyone except for Queen Blossom, that is!

"Hear ye, hear ye!" Scribblehopper cried.

We're all here... except the queen!

BLOSSOM, QUEEN OF THE FAIRIES: ABSENT!

SIR GERONIMO OF STILTON, FEARLESS KNIGHT: PRESENT!

BLUE RIDER, REPRESENTATIVE OF THE KNIGHTS: PRESENT!

WIZARD LAKENESS, FIRST ADVISOR TO THE QUEEN: PRESENT!

PRINCESS BITSY LUCKYBUG, REPRESENTATIVE OF THE FLYING CREATURES: PRESENT!

QUEEN COZY, REPRESENTATIVE OF THE GNOMES: PRESENT!

BLIZZARD, REPRESENTATIVE OF THE FOUR-LEGGED CREATURES: PRESENT!

PRINCESS EMERALD, REPRESENTATIVE OF THE ELVES: PRESENT!

STRONGHEART, REPRESENTATIVE OF THE GIANTS: PRESENT!

CORALINE, REPRESENTATIVE OF THE FAIRY ACADEMY: PRESENT!

CHATTERCLAWS, REPRESENTATIVE OF THE SEA CREATURES: PRESENT!

KING CHUCKLES, REPRESENTATIVE OF THE PIXIES: PRESENT!

KING TYLER TERRAIN, REPRESENTATIVE OF THE UNDERGROUND DWELLERS: PRESENT!

Hear ye, hear ye!

"I, SCRIBBLEHOPPER, the honorary secretary of the Council of the Thirteen Sages, officially call this meeting to order. Today we will discuss four terrible DISAPPEARANCES: our beloved queen, Blossom; *The Book of a Thousand Spells*; the Crystal Sphere; and the Whispering Wand! I have composed an epic p —"

Blue Rider cut off Scribblehopper before he ended up **talking** for hours. "Welcome, honorable sages," Blue Rider began. "We are lucky to be joined by Sir Geronimo of Stilton. Let's discuss how he can **HELP**!"

All the sages began to propose ideas at once. Each one sounded more **DANGEROUS** than the last. Yikes! I may be a knight, but I'm also a real scaredy-mouse!

"Knight, you should search for Blossom at the bottom of the sea . . ."

"Knight, you should explore the Woods of the Snarling Witches in search of our queen . . ."

"Knight, maybe you can tame a **WILD DRAGON** and fly over the entire Kingdom of Fantasy looking for Blossom . . ."

Luckily, at that point, Cozy, Queen of the Gnomes, stood up.

"Sages, this knight **COULD** do many of these things," she said solemnly. "But we all know there is one thing he **must** do: Find the Invisible Cloak! It will help him hide from his enemies on his way to find Blossom!"

"But where will I find this cloak?" I asked.

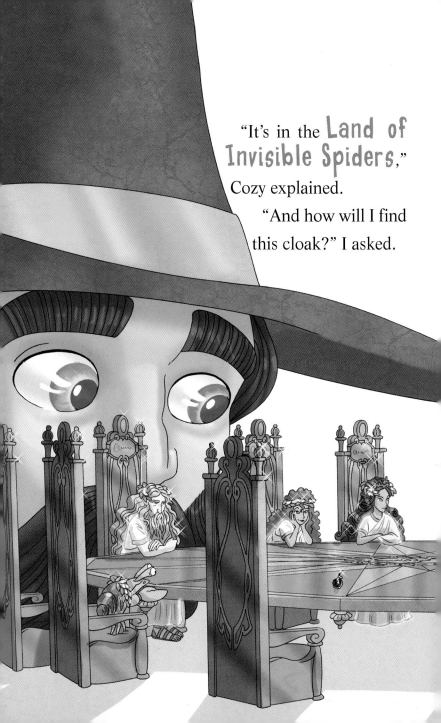

"It's in the Land of Invisible Spiders," Cozy explained.

"And how will I find this cloak?" I asked.

"You'll look for it, of course!" Cozy explained.

"But *how* will I look for it if it's INVISIBLE?" I asked, confused.

Cozy just shrugged.

"I don't know," she replied. "I'm not the knight — you are! FIGURE IT OUT!"

Scribblehopper poked me with his goose-feather pen.

Knight, you must find the Invisible Cloak!

"Come on, Knight!" he yelled. "What's with all the questions? We all know you have a **secret PLaN** to save the Kingdom of Fantasy, right?"

"Oh, a secret plan," the sages muttered, **impressed**. "We're counting on you, Knight! You're our **only hope**!"

Cheese and crackers! A secret plan? I had no secret plan. Other than secretly wishing I was back home, reading in my cozy chair! But I had to say something.

"Dear friends," I announced. "Um, of course I will have a **PLAN**. And I'd like to have a plan sooner rather than later. But for now, it might be LATER! Or maybe it will be **SOONER**. Who knows? But since it must be a secret, I will keep my plan to myself!"

The sages bowed their heads in awe and admiration.

"Oh, Knight, you are so wise!"

Moldy mozzarella! I wasn't wise. In fact, I didn't have any idea what I was doing!

"Well, since the knight knows what he's doing, then this meeting of the Council of the Thirteen Sages is adjourned. Everyone proceed to the GREAT BANQUET!"

"Yay!" everyone shouted. "Time to eat!"

The sages all got up and headed down the secret passageway toward the **BANQUET HALL**.

This meeting of the Council of the Thirteen Sages is adjourned!

ALGAE CRACKERS AND CLAM JAM!

The banquet hall was set with a very long table covered with a white **tablecloth** that had been woven by fairies and embroidered with a delicate **ROSE** print.

Dishes of delicious breakfast foods covered the table. There were warm, fresh **pastries**; soft, fresh **BREADS**; creamy spreads; and sweet jellies and jams. There were vats of **FRESHLY SQUEEZED** orange juice, bottles of fresh milk, and kettles of hot, fragrant **tea**.

I tried to grab a cheesy pastry, but Chatterclaws **PINCHED** me, knocking the delicious treat right out of my paws.

"What are you doing, Sir Whatsit?" he scolded me. "You're about to leave on a very long journey. You should eat something healthy!"

Then he handed me a plate of **algae crackers** with **clam jam** on them and a sludgy smoothie that smelled like seawater.

TYPICAL HERMIT CRAB BREAKFAST

Yum!

Delicacies in the Land of Hermit Crabs
The main ingredient in hermit crab cuisine is algae. Some of the delicious dishes that can be prepared with algae include: ocean-floor soup, lichen-and-algae dumplings, algae-and-green-fly soufflé, algae-stuffed pastries, and seawater smoothies.

Chatterclaws's mother, a celebrated chef in the Land of Hermit Crabs

"My **MOTHER** made this food with her own **CLAWS**," Chatterclaws explained. "She'll be very whatsitcalled — very offended if you don't eat every last bite!"

BLECH!

Luckily, Blue Rider came to my rescue.

"Knight, it's time to leave!" he said. "Here is your **armor** and a *pendant* with Blossom's seal on it. I prepared a horse for you and packed a sack with things you'll need on your trip, including a **map** and disguises."

"Thank you!" I told my friend gratefully.

"To save Blossom, you must first figure out who stole the three magical objects," he said to me. "You already found your first clue in Crystal

Castle: the strange **gold buckle**. Surely the **THIEF** left other clues!

"Go to the **EMPIRE OF THE RUBY DRAGONS** to search for clues about the Crystal Sphere. Then travel to the Kingdom of the Hissing Serpents to find clues about the Whispering Wand. But first, go to the Land of Invisible Spiders. You'll need to find and borrow the Invisible Cloak if you have any chance of making it back **ALIVE**. Chatterclaws will be your guide."

Chatterclaws passed me a plate of mussels in sewer sauce.

"Before we go, Knight, here's a little **snack**!"

For you, Knight!

How stinky!

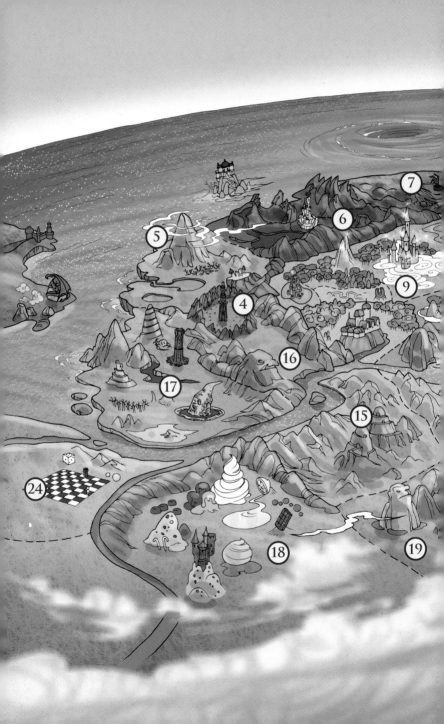

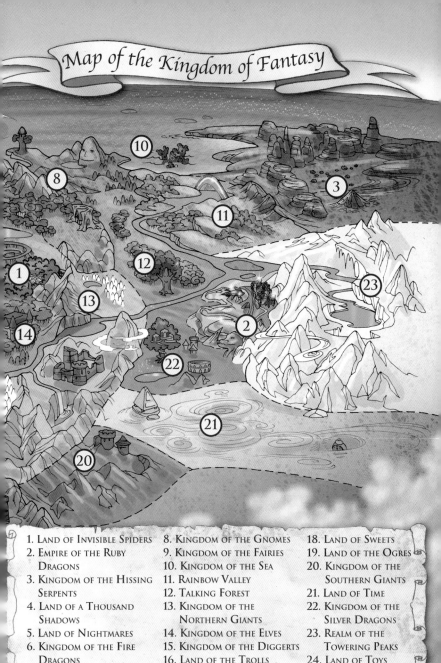

Map of the Kingdom of Fantasy

1. LAND OF INVISIBLE SPIDERS
2. EMPIRE OF THE RUBY DRAGONS
3. KINGDOM OF THE HISSING SERPENTS
4. LAND OF A THOUSAND SHADOWS
5. LAND OF NIGHTMARES
6. KINGDOM OF THE FIRE DRAGONS
7. KINGDOM OF THE PIXIES
8. KINGDOM OF THE GNOMES
9. KINGDOM OF THE FAIRIES
10. KINGDOM OF THE SEA
11. RAINBOW VALLEY
12. TALKING FOREST
13. KINGDOM OF THE NORTHERN GIANTS
14. KINGDOM OF THE ELVES
15. KINGDOM OF THE DIGGERTS
16. LAND OF THE TROLLS
17. KINGDOM OF THE WITCHES
18. LAND OF SWEETS
19. LAND OF THE OGRES
20. KINGDOM OF THE SOUTHERN GIANTS
21. LAND OF TIME
22. KINGDOM OF THE SILVER DRAGONS
23. REALM OF THE TOWERING PEAKS
24. LAND OF TOYS

BEWARE, KNIGHT!

Chatterclaws **pinched** my tail as I climbed on the horse.

"Let's go, Knight!" he urged me.

Creatures lined the road in front

He'll disappear, too!

Sob! Sob!

Oh, the poor knight!

Awooooo!

of Crystal Castle. Everyone in the crowd waved their handkerchiefs, crying for me.

"Oh, poor knight! Let's hope he lives!"

"Yes, let's hope he doesn't DISAPPEAR, too . . ."

"Let's say GOOD-BYE now in case we never see him again!"

I faced the crowd. "Umm, isn't there anyone who wants to come with me? You know, just to give me a helping paw in case I come across some **SCARY CREATURES** in the woods?"

Good luck!

Let's hope he doesn't disappear!

Good-bye!

See you soon, I hope!   Good-bye!

"Oh, no, Knight," came one reply. "You'll be just fine on your own."

"Plus we don't want to DISAPPEAR, too!" said another creature. "And you're a brave knight, anyway! You're not scared, are you?"

Of course I was scared! But I tried my best to pretend I wasn't.

"Scared? Me? Absolutely not!" I said, faking confidence. "Good-bye, everyone! And don't worry — I'll try not to disappear, unless it's under the Invisible Cloak!"

As I headed away from Crystal Castle, I came to an intersection of many roads. Street signs POINTED in all directions. But which way did I need to go? Toward the KINGDOM OF THE DRAGONS, the Kingdom of the Pixies, or the Kingdom of the Giants? I definitely didn't want to go toward the KINGDOM OF THE WITCHES.

My whiskers trembled just thinking about that **SCARY** place!

Unfortunately, I didn't see any sign for the Land of Invisible Spiders . . .

Luckily (or unluckily, depending on how you wanted to look at it), Chatterclaws started shouting directions in my ear.

"Turn left!" he SHRIEKED. "Now turn right! No, don't whatchamacallit, Knight. You need to go THIS way, do you understand? Not THAT way. If you go the

wrong way, remember that I told you not to!"

In the end, I decided to go east. And that's when it began. I heard a gurgling noise:

BLUB,
BLUB,
BLUB,
BLURG, BLURG, BLUB . . .
GRRRRROWWWWWL!
BLURG . . .

Moldy mozzarella! What was it? An evil creature?

Oops, nope! I realized it was the sound of my stomach.

"Oh no!" I groaned. "I had those mussels with

Help . . .

A bush!

sewer sauce. Chatterclaws, you **poisoned** me!"

I got down off the horse in a hurry and scurried behind a **bush**. I was there for quite a while!

Finally, I was feeling better, so I got back on the horse. But five minutes later, my stomach was gurgling again. *Oh, I felt awful!*

Eventually I was able to get back on the horse, and we finally left the thick forest that surrounded the fairy city.

What a stomachache!

Come on, Knight!

I feel awful!

WANTED: DEAD OR ALIVE!

We trotted into a cute little village. I quickly noticed signs hanging everywhere. They were on the wall of an **INN**, on the door to a **BARN** — there was even one hanging on an **oak** tree!

What could those signs be saying? As I rode CLOSeR, I took a better look at the snout pictured on the signs. It looked oddly familiar . . .

Wait a minute — *it was me!*

I read the text on the sign. Can you translate it?*

*You can find the Fantasian Alphabet on page 310.

It said: "Wanted: Dead or Alive!"

Holey cheese! Those signs meant that someone wanted me dead or alive! Someone was really out to get me. But WHO could it be?

"Oh no," Chatterclaws moaned. "Someone's looking for you, Knight — *dead* or ALIVE! And if you're in danger, then I am, t —"

THUMP! Chatterclaws had fainted.

I quickly sprayed him with some seawater I found in the bag Blue Rider had packed for me.

Here's some seawater!

Ugh!

"Knight!" Chatterclaws cried as soon as he woke. "Our enemies are on our trail!"

We decided it was best to split up to cover our tracks. Chatterclaws returned to Crystal Castle on my horse while I **hid** behind a bush. I took out one of the disguises that Blue Rider had packed in my bag. Soon I was dressed as an **old lady**. When night fell, I continued my **JOURNEY**. I was **deep** in the dark forest when I met a group of

Good-bye!

See you soon!

thirteen Stinging Pixies. They carried a pair of giant SILVER SCISSORS.

"Hey, old lady." They giggled. "Have you seen a MOUSE dressed like a knight?"

I did my best to imitate the voice of a little old lady:

"N-no, no, no, I haven't," I squeaked. "why do you ask?"

No, no, no, I haven't!

Did you see a mouse dressed like a knight?

Ha, ha, ha!

Hee, hee, hee!

"Because the wizard Longbeard put a bounty on his tail of thirty gold coins." They snickered.

The pixies continued through the forest, singing as they went:

"Snip, snip, never fail!
If we find that mouse, we'll chop off his tail"

Yikes! Suddenly, the ground began to **shake** and a strong **stench** filled the air.

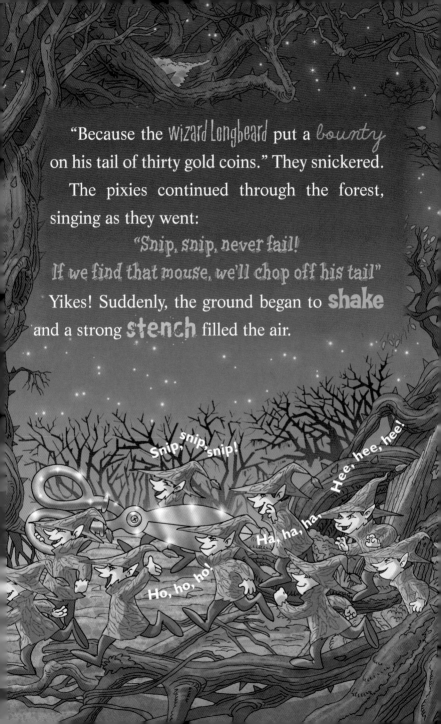

A GIGANTIC OGRE'S FOOT! (IT SMELLS AS BAD AS IT LOOKS!)

Crusty cat litter! What now?

I rounded a bend in the woods and came snout-to-foot with a gigantic ogre. He was carrying an enormouse wooden club.

Holey cheese!

"Hey, you!" he thundered. "Have you seen an itsy-bitsy little knight?"

"**NO, NO, NO,**" I squeaked in my old-lady voice. "I haven't seen any knights!"

"I'm sure I'll find him up ahead," the ogre grumbled at me. "I just know he's on this road!"

He walked away, the ground **SHAKING** as he went.

As soon as he was far away, I began to run through the forest. I was hoping to find directions to the Land of Invisible Spiders. But instead I came across another traveler. It was a wolf with a **mangled** ear and a knife in his belt. He was wearing a dark hooded tunic and he leaned on a *knotted* cane.

It was **Robin of the woods**, one of the most famouse outlaws in the kingdom!

"Good evening, **MADAM**," the wolf greeted me. "You haven't seen a knight, have you?"

"**NO, NO, NO,**" I answered in my trembling old-lady voice. "I haven't seen any knights!"

"And mice?" he insisted. "Have you seen any mice?"

"**NO, NO, NO,**" I squeaked. "No mice, either. Sorry!"

Robin of the Woods

This wolf is one of the most well-known outlaws in the Kingdom of Fantasy. You can recognize Robin easily because of his mangled left ear. His main competition is Ranger, the Coyote of Danger, who is part of the Band of Seven Thieves.

"Hmmm," he replied, looking at me closely. "What about a mouse dressed in a disguise so he won't be noticed? Have you seen one of those?"

"N-n-no!" I stammered. "I haven't seen anyone!"

He eyed me suspiciously.

"Why are you trembling, old lady?" he asked.

"Um, i-it's because I-I'm very c-cold!" I stuttered. "And very old! At my age this night air is the worst! And my arthritis is really killing me . . ."

The wolf FINALLY seemed to believe me.

"You're right," he agreed, pulling his cloak tighter around him. "It's very chilly tonight. Have a safe journey!"

I waited until the wolf was far, far away . . .

And then I fainted!

The first thing I thought when I woke up was this:

How would I ever make it to the mysterious Land of Invisible Spiders?

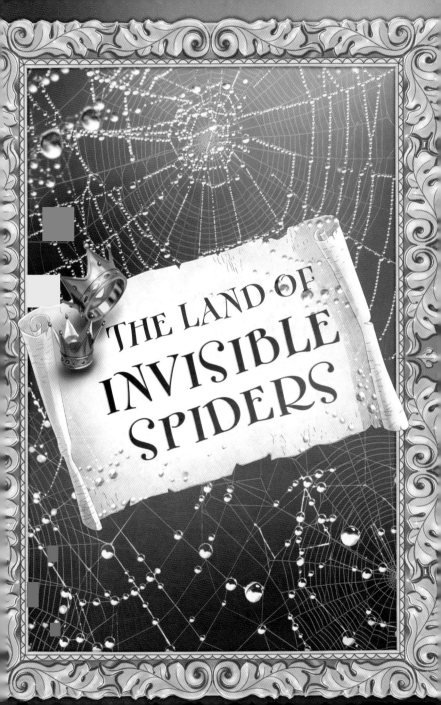

THE LAND OF
INVISIBLE
SPIDERS

THE SECRET OF THE INVISIBLE SPIDERS

I stopped to take a look at my map. I was hoping I could figure out how to get to the Land of Invisible Spiders on my own. Suddenly, I heard soft voices whispering together:

"SPIDERS, SPIDERS, SPIDERS ARE WEEEEE! WEAVING TOGETHER: ONE, TWO, THREEEEEE! WE ARE SPIDERS THAT YOU'LL NEVER SEEEEEE!"

Without even realizing it, I had arrived! But how would I ever find the Invisible Cloak if I couldn't see the spiders? I figured the best thing to do was to tell the **TRUTH**.

"Hello, invisible spiders!" I said loudly. "I may seem like an old lady, but I am actually Sir Geronimo of Stilton, a rodent **knight**. I am here to ask to **BORROW** the Invisible Cloak. I need it because I am on a very important mission to save the *Kingdom of Fantasy*!"

As soon as I finished squeaking, there was a moment of silence followed by a chorus of laughter.

HA, HA, HA! HA, HA, HA! HA, HA, HA!
HEE, HEE, HEE! HEE, HEE, HEE!
HO, HO, HO! HO, HO, HO! HO, HO, HO!

Holey cheese! The invisible spiders were **laughing** at me!

"This mouse can't even **SEE** us!" the spiders twittered.

The spiders even made up a little song about me right on the spot!

"YOU SAY YOU'RE A KNIGHT,
BUT YOU LOOK VERY OLD.
IN ANY CASE,
YOU'RE REALLY QUITE BOLD!
YOU ASK FOR A CLOAK
THAT YOU CAN'T EVEN SEE.
WHAT MAKES YOU THINK
YOU CAN TAKE IT FOR FREE?"

Then they started giggling again. I was really getting annoyed.

"**Enough!**" I yelled. "I'm sorry, but it's not nice to laugh at me like that!"

Finally, a serious voice spoke up.

"Hello, traveler," the voice said. "Are you really who you say you are? Are you really the knight sent to save *Queen Blossom*?"

I raised the **PENDANT** with Blossom's seal on it.

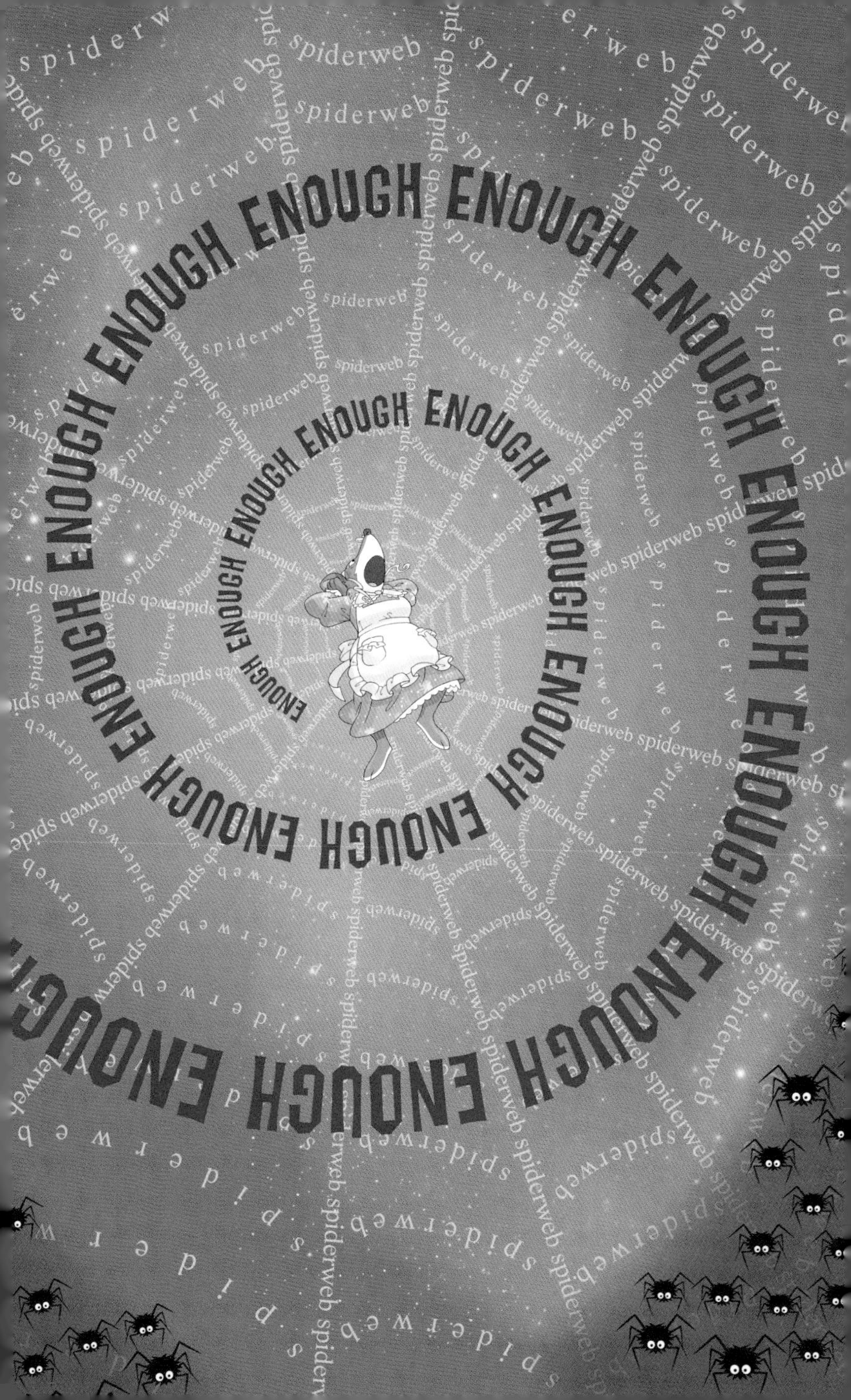

"Here is the **royal seal** that proves it," I explained. "Now will you please **help** me? There's no time to waste! Blossom is in danger."

"Yes, of course we will help," the voice replied. "But if you want to see us, you must first pass a *test of courage* and let us sting you! Only then will you be able to **see** us and receive our help."

I hesitated. I didn't want to be **STUNG**! What if it hurt? But I really had no choice.

"Okay, okay," I said, trying to sound **BRAVE**.

What?

The Secret of the Invisible Spiders
These spiders are invisible to all but those who have been stung.

THE LAND OF INVISIBLE SPIDERS

The **INVISIBLE SPIDERS** have round, furry bodies and long legs. They move very quickly, and their racing championships are very famouse! They hardly ever sting anyone because they are invisible and so they usually don't need to defend themselves.

The spiders rarely let outsiders into their world. When they do, the outsider must pass a test of courage. Once stung, a creature will have a few drops of spider venom in his body. This will allow him to see the mysterious land and its inhabitants.

The **INVISIBLE SPIDERS** are pranksters who love playing tricks on travelers and telling jokes. Their greatest treasure is the Invisible Cloak. It took seven generations for the spiders to weave the cloak using a top secret weaving method! Their **KING** and **QUEEN** are elected based on their intelligence, wisdom, and generosity to others.

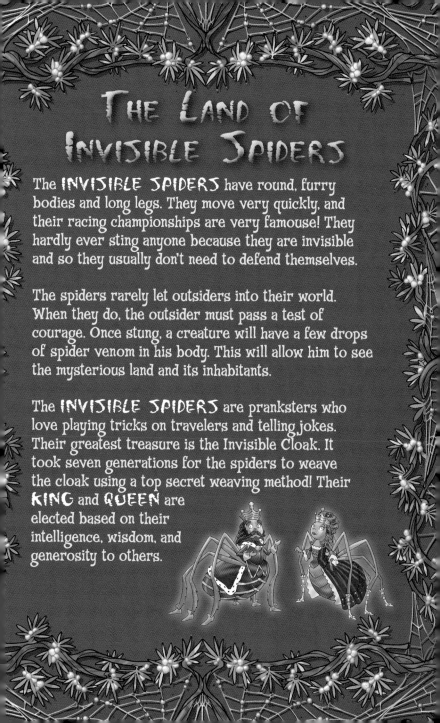

"Go ahead and sting me if you must!"

A moment later, I felt something hairy climbing up my arm. Then I felt a SHARP sting.

"Ouchie!" I shrieked.

It felt as if lightning had struck me. Then a wave of heat washed over me. I closed my eyes and my head began to **spin and spin and spin**. When I opened my eyes again, I realized I had shrunk down to the size of a spider. A giant juniper tree with twisted branches loomed in front of me.

The trunk had scorches and burn marks all over it. Spiderwebs of many shapes and sizes covered the branches. In the center of the tree there was a huge **spiderweb**

made from golden thread. A spider wearing a **crown** sat in the middle of it.

Here I am, Knight!

"Can you see me now, Knight?" he asked.

I nodded.

"I was the one speaking to you earlier," he explained. "I am **King Longlegs the Thirteenth**, also known as the Great Master of Weaving, Lord of the Longthread, and the Hairy-Legged Emperor. Welcome!"

Now I see you!

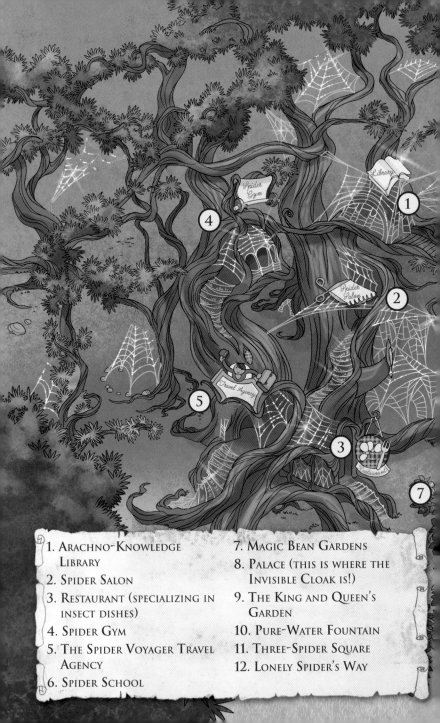

1. Arachno-Knowledge Library
2. Spider Salon
3. Restaurant (specializing in insect dishes)
4. Spider Gym
5. The Spider Voyager Travel Agency
6. Spider School
7. Magic Bean Gardens
8. Palace (this is where the Invisible Cloak is!)
9. The King and Queen's Garden
10. Pure-Water Fountain
11. Three-Spider Square
12. Lonely Spider's Way

The Land of Invisible Spiders

KING LONGLEGS AND QUEEN SPINDERELLA

With a flick of a leg, King Longlegs gestured for me to follow him. We walked down a long, dark, damp path among the **juniper trees**.

We went LOWER and LOWER until we were in a vast cavern under a tree. Roots hung from the ceiling, and the walls were decorated with round white stones. Each stone was engraved with an image of a crown and the names of a king and queen who had ruled the land.

The last stone on the wall had the names **Longlegs** and **Spinderella** written on it.

King Longlegs sat down on one of two golden spider-shape thrones.

"Knight, what can the invisible spiders do for you?" he asked.

"I need to borrow the **Invisible Cloak**," I explained. "Someone is after me, and I need the cloak to help hide me from my **enemies** so I can complete my mission!"

THE SOLUTION
IS ON PAGE 511.

King Longlegs was quiet for a moment.

"**Knight**, the cloak is our most precious **treasure**," he explained. "**Seven generations** of spiders worked day and night to complete it. They wove it with their saliva, which makes extremely sturdy thread. The final result is completely invisible!"

He sighed.

"But if you need the cloak to **save** Queen Blossom, we will loan him to you," he said. "We want to help you complete your **mission**."

At that moment, another spider wearing a gold crown appeared. She was surrounded by a group of lady spiders wearing *lacy*, *colorful* dresses.

"Ooooh, Knight, is it true?" she asked. "Have

you really come to take away our beloved little cloak?"

"This is my wife, Queen Spinderella," Longlegs explained. "The cloak is very **dear** to her . . ."

The queen sobbed. Her spider tears were flying left and right.

"Poor, poor, poor cloak," she cried. "So young and defenseless and forced to travel to distant lands . . ."

"Come now, Spinderella," King Longlegs told his wife. "The knight will take good care of our cloak."

"Oh, Knight!" The queen turned to me. "You'll treat him well, won't you? Please promise me, Knight. The invisible spiders LOVE our Invisible Cloak and we don't want anything to happen to him!"

I didn't understand why everyone called the cloak "him." Still, I tried to reassure her.

"Of course I will treat it — er, him — well, Your Majesty," I said.

King Longlegs signaled to a band of spider guards armed with lances dipped in SPIDER VENOM.

"Bring the Invisible Cloak here at once!" he ordered.

"Yes, Your Majesty!" they replied before they scampered away.

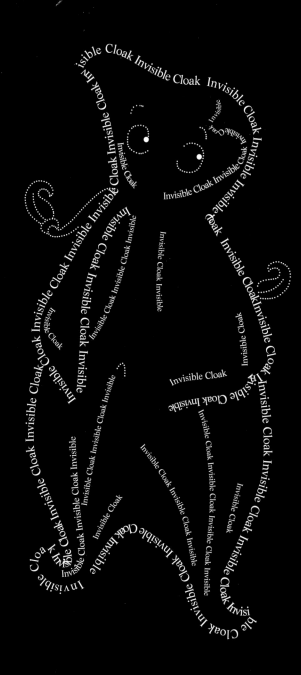

THE MYSTERIOUS
INVISIBLE CLOAK

A short while later, the spider guards returned carrying a **SEDAN CHAIR**.

"So, Knight, what do you say?" King Longlegs asked me proudly. "What do you think of our *amazing* Invisible Cloak?"

I stared at the empty sedan chair.

"Um, honestly, I don't see **ANYTHING**," I told the king. "I don't see the cloak at all!"

He burst out laughing.

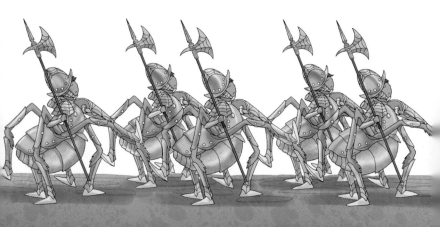

"Ha, ha, ha!" he chuckled. "The knight says he doesn't see the Invisible Cloak!"

The whole court laughed along with him.

"Ha, ha, ha!" The spiders giggled. "He says he doesn't see the cloak . . ."

Even the queen stopped sobbing for a moment.

"Ha, ha, ha!" she laughed. "He says he doesn't see the cloak. Hee, hee, hee!"

All of the invisible spiders who had crowded into the assembly room burst out laughing.

"HA, HA, HAAAAAAA! THE KNIGHT DOESN'T SEE THE CLOAK!"

Tee-hee!

Hee, hee, hee!

Ho, ho, ho!

Hee, hee, hee!

Ha, ha, ha!

Ha, ha, ha!

Ho, ho, ho!

Right at that moment someone let out a little toot: PFFFFT!

Everyone laughed even more.

"Ha, ha, ha! Hee, hee, hee! Ho, ho, ho!"

The spiders **rolled** around their webs, GIGGLING. Some of them hung from their invisible threads, holding their stomachs from laughing so much.

What was so funny?

A tiny spider ran past me.

"Hey, silly knight," he teased me. "The cloak is there, but you can't see it because it's invisible! That's why it's called the Invisible Cloak, silly! You can't see the cloak — but

Ha,
ha,
ha!

Hee,
hee,
hee!

Ha,
ha,
ha!

Ho,
ho,
ho!

Hee,
hee,
hee!

Ho,
ho,
ho!

Ho,
ho,
ho!

Ho,
ho,
ho!

you can **smell him**, that's for sure!"

King Longlegs was crying from laughing so hard. He dried his **tears** and went toward the sedan chair. Then he took something from the chair and placed it in my paw. I couldn't SEE a thing, but I **felt** something soft against my fur.

"Tee-hee!" the thing in my paw snickered.

"Yikes!" I yelled, stunned. The Invisible Cloak **talked**?

Then I smelled an awful stench. The Invisible Cloak didn't just

Whew! That smells!

talk — he apparently also passed gas!

The invisible spiders all began laughing their heads off again.

"How many times have I told you not to do that when we have GUESTS?" Queen Spinderella scolded the cloak. Then she lowered her voice and spoke more **tenderly**.

"My dear little Cloak, the knight needs you to go with him," she explained. "Will you do it, SWEETIE?"

"Tee-hee! Tee-hee! Tee-hee!" The cloak giggled and whispered something to the queen.

The queen turned to me.

"The Invisible Cloak says you seem a little silly, but he likes you anyway," she said. "He says he'll **GO**!"

The spiders all cheered.

"Knight, only those who have the right amount of spider venom in their veins can see the Invisible Cloak," King Longlegs explained. "If you would like to see him, you must let me sting you once more. Are you willing to undergo another *test of courage* to save the Kingdom of Fantasy?"

I began trembling from the end of my tail all the way up to the tips of my whiskers. Not another STiNg! But then I thought of sweet Queen Blossom and how much she — and the entire kingdom — needed me.

"I'll do it!" I said bravely.

Then I closed my eyes and the spider king stung me again. When I opened my eyes, a cloak with a GOOFY smile floated in front of me. It was the mysterious Invisible Cloak!

Tee-hee!

THE INVISIBLE CLOAK

HIS STORY
He was woven by seven generations of spiders who used special invisible thread made from their *spider saliva*.

CHARACTERISTICS
The cloak is shaped like a rectangle and as soft and weightless as the *breeze*. He is as invisible as a **ghost** at midnight!

USES
He can become a cloak, a scarf, or a blanket as necessary, and he can be used to protect from the RAIN or the SUN. In an emergency, the cloak can be used as a **flying carpet** or as a *rope* to climb up or down a cliff. The cloak can be used to make someone invisible, but he can also hide objects. Just wrap them in the cloak!

WARNINGS
Any creature wrapped in the cloak will become invisible, but if a body part is sticking out, that part will still be visible! When the cloak moves, it makes a RUSTLING sound. This sound is the only clue to the cloak's presence.

BEHAVIORS

The cloak is friendly and eager to please. But if he feels neglected, he becomes surly and grumpy. If he gets really offended, he may DISAPPEAR! The only way to find him is by listening for the rustling sound. Or you can offer him some beans to eat, and then you'll find him right away because of the smell!

PASSIONS

He loves INVISIBLE BEANS, but don't give him too many or he'll be tooting all day long! Three beans a day are plenty. More than that and the stench will be unbearable. If you're going to be spending a lot of time with him, you might want to invest in nose plugs!

FAVORITE PHRASES

Here are some things he likes to say:

"Tee-hee-hee! You can't catch me!"

"You can't see me, but you sure can smell me!"

"I won't be mean if you give me a bean!"

"It wasn't me! . . . Or was it?"

HOW TO CARE FOR THE INVISIBLE CLOAK

1 The Invisible Cloak must be brushed three times a day with a special brush made from blue unicorn hair.

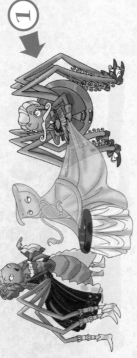

2 The Invisible Cloak can be washed only in cool water with fragrance-free soap.

3 Be careful not to rip or pull any of the cloak's threads!

Invisible bean

(5)

(4) Tie a leash made of golden silk around the Invisible Cloak and around your wrist so you don't lose him on walks.

Be sure to feed the Invisible Cloak his favorite food — invisible beans! But don't feed him more than three beans a day. If you do, you'll be sorry!

TRAVELING WITH THE INVISIBLE CLOAK

After Queen Spinderella had finished telling me how to care for the cloak, she handed me a rolled-up scroll. It was stamped with a wax seal showing the crest of the Land of Invisible Spiders.

"This will be a reminder in case you **forget** anything," she explained.

Here are the instructions!

Then she gave me a small bag made of PURPLE silk. It was embroidered with gold letters that read: "Invisible beans for the Invisible Cloak." Below that in smaller letters it read: "**WARNING**: Do **NOT** use more than ***three*** a day!"

"Be **careful** with those beans, Knight!" she said with a chuckle. "Our cloak can be quite a little stinker!"

Beans

Finally, she gave me a pair of **golden nose plugs**.

"You'll need these," she said. "Put these on when you can't take it anymore."

Purple silk bag

I didn't even have a chance to try out the nose plugs before the cloak let another one rip.

PFFFFT!

Golden nose plugs

Everyone laughed their heads off:

"Ha, ha, ha! Hee, hee, hee! Ho, ho, ho! The cloak . . . the beans . . . the smell. **Poor Knight!**"

How stinky! Ha, ha, ha! Hee, hee, hee! Ho, ho, ho! Ha, ha, ha!

It was time to leave. I probably wouldn't need my old-lady DISGUISE anymore now that I had the Invisible Cloak. But I left it on just to be safe.

The spiders WAVED good-bye with their many legs.

"Farewell, Knight!" they called out. "Have a good trip!"

"Thank you, everyone," I replied. "And thank you especially for the Invisible Cloak!"

"Tee-hee-hee!" the cloak snickered when he heard his name. "Good-bye, everyone! And remember: You can't see me, but you sure can smell me!"

Then he wiggled happily, letting out another stink bomb. This time I was quick to plug my nose, but the spiders couldn't stop laughing. They found the whole thing *hilarious*!

Oh, how do I always get myself into these messes?

That was how I headed down the path of silver stones in the company of the stinky Invisible Cloak. We were on our way to the **EMPIRE OF THE RUBY DRAGONS** to find clues about the Crystal Sphere!

After just a few steps, I returned to my normal size.

Then I walked and walked and walked and walked and walked and walked for hours and hours and hours and hours and hours and hours and hours and hours.

Finally the path began to go **DOWN AND DOWN AND DOWN.**

The path took me right into a bunch of **thorny** bushes. As I continued down the road, the bushes

became taller and taller and thicker and thornier!
And then one of the thorns **poked** me!

OUCHIE! My poor tail!

Then I heard a loud RIIIPPPP!

HOLEY CHEESE! The thorns had ripped the
Invisible Cloak! NOOOOOOOO!

I couldn't believe my bad luck. The poor
Invisible Cloak began to CRY.

"Waaa!" he whimpered. "I want to go home!"

I Sell It All!

A raspy **CAW** began to drown out the Invisible Cloak's sobs.

"Magical objects for sale!" the voice called out. "**I SELL IT ALL!** Dragon-fire extinguishers? Got 'em! Nail clippers for *giants*? Of course! Anti-wrinkle cream for witches? You bet! *Perfume* for trolls? Step right up! I sell it all . . . and much, much more! **CAWWW!**"

I looked around to see where the voice was coming from. Above me, a **RAVEN** was perched in a tree. As soon as he saw me, the raven cawed happily.

Nail clippers for giants

Dragon-fire extinguishers

Perfume for trolls

Anti-wrinkle cream for witches

Pick-axes for gnome

"Goody!" he exclaimed. "A client!"

Then he opened the trunk around his neck.

"What do you **NEED**, miss?" he asked. "Cleverwing has everything . . . and much, much more. **CAWWW!**"

"I need something to repair . . . um . . . an INVISIBLE object!" I explained.

The raven looked at me carefully.

I sell it all!

"An INVISIBLE object?" he asked.

I tried to be as vague as possible. I wasn't sure I could trust him, but I had **NO CHOICE**.

"Well, yes. Um, it's an object that is invisible," I explained. "It's ripped."

CLEVERWING

ALSO KNOWN AS
THE MASTER OF CLEVERNESS

WHO HE IS:
Cleverwing is the slyest raven in the Kingdom of Fantasy. He comes from the only family of ravens in the kingdom that is still faithful to Blossom. All the other ravens have aligned themselves with the witches!

WHAT HE DOES:
He sells just about everything. He keeps his merchandise in a chest that he always wears around his neck.

WARNINGS:
Cleverwing isn't evil, but don't trust him: He is very sly! If you meet him, he will surely try to take advantage of you by selling you something you don't need, or by tricking you into signing some suspicious contract.

"So . . . it's something woven?" he asked **EXCITEDLY**. "It's the Invisible Cloak, isn't it?" He hopped eagerly. "There are so many legends about it, but I didn't believe that it really existed! **CAWWW!**"

I didn't want to admit that I had the cloak, but what could I do?

"Well, you see — uh, yes, you could define it like that," I stammered.

He PINCHED my ear.

"You sly old lady!" he teased. "You tore that precious cloak and now you have to fix it, huh? Well, don't worry! Today is your lucky day! I have everything and more! What do you need to mend an Invisible Cloak? Well, that's obvious: you need a NeeDLe and invisible thread!

Then he rummaged through his chest until he pulled something out and placed

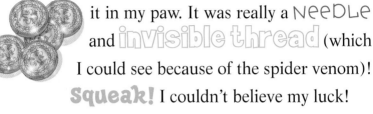

it in my paw. It was really a Needle and invisible thread (which I could see because of the spider venom)! Squeak! I couldn't believe my luck!

"And how must does this cost?" I asked.

"I'll give you a special price," he replied with a wink. "Just five gold coins. CAWWW!"

"What?!" I protested. "But I don't have that much!"

"Oh, really?" he replied slyly. "Is that too much? Well, never mind, then. Best wishes, ma'am. CAWWW!"

"But the cloak is really suffering," I explained. The raven shrugged.

"Sorry, business is business. CAWWW!"

I tried once more. "What if I paid you five gold coins after I complete my mission and return to Crystal Castle?"

The raven thought about it for a moment. Then

he pulled out a **scroll**, a bottle of **ink**, and a goose-feather **pen**.

"I'm feeling generous today," Cleverwing said. "Sign this contract that says you will give me **five gold coins** plus **ten coins** in interest per day, and I will sell you the needle and thread!"

I had no other choice, so I signed it. He patted me on the back with his wing.

"Now, to be sure you pay me, I will follow you all the way to CRYSTAL CASTLE."

Suddenly, his eye fell on one of the WANTED signs with my snout on it.

"Wait a minute!" he squawked.

He hopped over to the sign, pulled a **red** pen out of his pocket, and drew hair in a bun and a frilly collar on the picture before he turned back to me.

"Come now, confess!" he told me. "You're not an old lady — you are the **fearless knight**!"

I couldn't hide my true identity any longer.

"Yes, it's true," I replied. "It's me!"

I took off my old-lady disguise.

"Hmmm," the raven mused. "I wonder what I should do. On the one wing, I want to report you! I'll get a lot of gold coins. But on the

other wing, if I report you, I won't get the five gold coins you owe me — plus the ten coins in interest per day! Let's do this: I'll report you, but only after we get to Crystal Castle. That way you'll have paid me the five gold coins — plus the ten coins in interest per day! — and I can get the reward, too. Do you see how clever I am? CAWWW!"

Two Unbearable Travel Companions

I took the NEEDLE and thread that had cost me so much and mended the Invisible Cloak. Of course the cloak complained the entire time, but as soon as I finished, he cheered up again.

Then the raven pecked me with his beak.

"Let's go, mouse!" he squawked. "The **sooner** we get going, the **sooner** you'll complete your mission. And then I'll get my gold! CAWWW!"

Waa! Ouchie!

Come on, let's go!

But before we could leave, the cloak tugged at my sleeve.

"Please don't be MEAN, Knight!" he begged. "Give me a **bean**! I'm so hungry."

I gave him a bean just to keep him **quiet**. But I was immediately assaulted by the most terrible odor.

"**CAWWW!**" the raven cried. "That stinks!"

I couldn't concentrate with all their complaining.

"Enough!" I squeaked. "I can't think straight!"

They quieted down while I consulted the map. To get to the Empire of the Ruby Dragons from where we were, we needed to scale an enormouse **mountain**, climb a **glacier**, and cross a raging **river**.

Holey cheese! We would never make it!

"Hey, you know I can fly, right?" the cloak reminded me.

"Of course!" I squeaked. "Why didn't I think of

that? We will **fly** on the Invisible Cloak!"

"Where you go, I go," the raven squawked. "Understand? I want my money! CAWWW!"

I sat on the cloak, and Cleverwing made himself comfortable next to me.

"I may have wings, but I don't mind **resting** them for a while," he said. "That way you won't get any ideas about disappearing, mouse!"

Even after the cloak took off, the raven continued squawking.

"That's it?" he complained. "Ravens can fly much better than this. CAWWW!"

The cloak responded by making three **bone-chilling** spins.

"**HEEEEELP!**" I squeaked. "I'm too fond of my fur!"

But the raven wasn't impressed.

"You think that's a big deal?" he heckled the cloak. "I know how to fly, too, you know! I've

Oh no!

The cloak went upward

Then he did a nosedive!

Heeeeelp!

I held on in terror!

Gulp!

been flying since I was born. **CAWWW!**"

The cloak did another nosedive, spiraling downward in a corkscrew.

I shrieked in fright!

"Where did you get your **FLYER'S LICENSE**?" the raven squawked. "Even a tiny, newly hatched raven can fly better than you!"

What a terrible trip! I had never been with two such unpleasant travel companions. Cleverwings **pecked** at the cloak and teased him constantly.

"Even a quail with his wing in a cast could fly *faster* than you!" Cleverwing cawed.

The offended cloak began to **TOOT** nonstop. I was forced to keep my nose plugs on the whole time, while the raven fanned the air with his wings.

"Phew!" he squawked. "Where did you ever find this stink bomb? He smells worse than a rotten egg! **CAWWW!**"

It was then that I realized the bag with the **invisible beans** was almost empty. That's why the cloak was so smelly!

It's almost empty!

"Why did you eat so many beans?" I scolded him. But by then it was too late. The rest of our journey to the Empire of the Ruby Dragons was a real **stinkfest**!

We flew . . . and flew . . . and flew . . . and flew . . . and flew . . . and flew . . . and flew . . . and flew . . . and flew . . .

As we flew, the birds around us kept **fainting** from the horrible stench!

At dawn on the third day, the raven spotted our destination.

THE POOR BIRDS KEPT FAINTING
FROM THE CLOAK'S STENCH!

We flew . . . and flew . . . and flew . . . all the way to the Empire of the Ruby Dragons!

Huh?

"CAWWW!" he squawked. "There it is: THE EMPIRE OF THE RUBY DRAGONS!"

The cloak turned and descended in a perilous nosedive as I held on, terrified.

"Please SLOW DOWN!" I squeaked. "I don't want to lose my fur!"

In response, the cloak did a triple spin and a backward somersault before finally landing on the ground. I thought I might toss my cheese, but . . .

WE HAD ARRIVED!

THE EMPIRE OF THE RUBY DRAGONS

HAVE YOU EVER SEEN A RUBY DRAGON?

I had never been **happier** to put my paws on firm ground. My stomach was all twisted up like a sock, and I felt so sick I thought I might TOSS MY CHEESE!

Cleverwing, on the other hand, quickly jumped down.

"Well that sure took a while, didn't it?" he crowed. "If I had **fLoWn**, we would have been here in the flap of a wing."

In response, the cloak TOOTED three times, just like a trumpet. Despite my nose plug, I nearly fainted.

"You might be an amateur when it comes to flying, but you sure are a professional when it comes to cutting the cheese!" the raven cawed as he waved a wing in front of his beak.

Ahead of us, a castle towered above a LUSH forest. As we got closer, I noticed that the walls, towers, and roof were a sparkling red color. The castle was made out of RUBIES!

When we arrived at the castle, I knocked timidly at the front door, which was ringed with rubies. What an impressive palace!

"Who's there?" replied a thunderous voice.

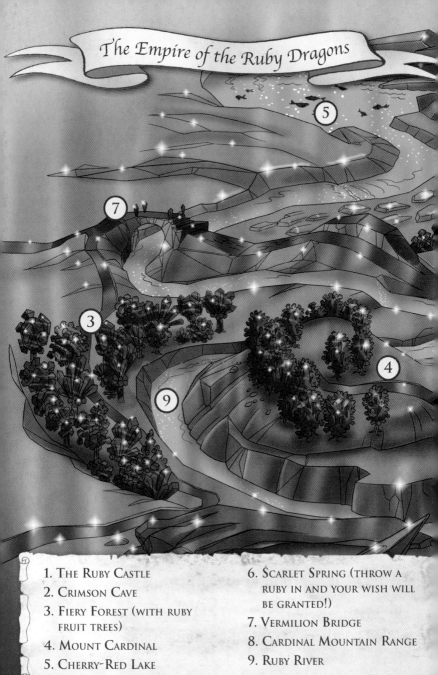

The Empire of the Ruby Dragons

1. THE RUBY CASTLE
2. CRIMSON CAVE
3. FIERY FOREST (WITH RUBY FRUIT TREES)
4. MOUNT CARDINAL
5. CHERRY-RED LAKE
6. SCARLET SPRING (THROW A RUBY IN AND YOUR WISH WILL BE GRANTED!)
7. VERMILION BRIDGE
8. CARDINAL MOUNTAIN RANGE
9. RUBY RIVER

"Um, I am S-Sir Geronimo of Stilton," I squeaked nervously. "I'm on a mission for Queen Blossom . . . uh, I mean I'm **searching** for Queen Blossom and the Crystal Sphere. You see, both of them are gone, and I'm looking for **clues**! We need to find them right away. It's very urgent!"

Holey cheese, I was **babbling** as if I were Chatterclaws!

The door **BURST** wide open. A red dragon three times my size **TOWERED** over me.

"For all the rubies in the kingdom!" the dragon shouted. "All you needed to say was that you are the **knight**! I know why you're here — I've been waiting for you! Come right in."

As I followed the dragon inside, I realized his claws, tail, and enormouse belly were all made from **RUBiES**! Even the scales on his back, his ears, and his teeth were **RUBiES**!

The dragon shook my paw (and almost crushed it!).

"By the way, I am Crimson Firetail. My dad is the King of the Ruby Dragons," he said. "Now let's hurry! Dinner's almost ready, and my mom will be upset if the soup is overcooked."

Suddenly, the cloak let out a real stinker.

"It wasn't me!" Crimson gasped, covering his ruby nostrils.

Toot!

Toot!

Toot!

Toot!

Toot!

"Whoever denied it supplied it," Cleverwing teased. "If you say it wasn't you, it probably was! CAWWW!"

What a stink!
It wasn't me!

The **DRAGON** slapped the ground angrily with his tail.

"Hey, Scrawny Wings!" he shouted. "Do you want me to turn you into **raven stew**?"

I could tell Cleverwing really wanted to peck the dragon with his **sharp** little beak.

"Stop!" I scolded him. "If you pick a fight with a dragon, I'll never complete my mission and you won't get your **GOLD** coins. Understand?"

Cleverwing calmed down immediately.

"**CAWWW!** Of course, the gold!" he squawked.

"My apologies, Sir Dragon," Cleverwing said, bowing to Crimson. "I didn't mean to offend you. It must have been the knight who cut the cheese! After all, he is a mouse. CAWWW!"

I was about to protest when I thought better of it. The dragon didn't know about the Invisible Cloak, and it seemed like a good idea to keep it that way, just in case.

"Um, yes, it was me," I admitted meekly. "So sorry!"

The dragon seemed appeased, and he signaled for us to follow him. We walked along a hallway paved with RUBIES, then turned down a passageway with RUBY walls. At the end was a RUBY door. We went inside and headed down another long RUBY hallway, emerging in a room with RUBY walls. Inside the room, two gigantic dragons sat on two RUBY thrones. It was KING AND QUEEN FIRETAIL!

THE DRAGON COURT

KING FIRETAIL

QUEEN FIRETAIL

CARMINE

CRIMSON

AUBURN

SCARLETT

The Ruby Castle

1. THRONE ROOM
2. THE THOUSAND-RUBY ROOM
3. GUEST ROOM
4. CRYSTAL SPHERE ROOM
5. WATCHTOWER
6. TRAINING GROUNDS
7. GUARD STATION
8. DRAGON-LANDING PLATFORM
9. SECRET PASSAGE

RUBY SOUP AND OTHER STRANGE THINGS

A crowd of DRAGONS surrounded the two leaders. A deep silence fell over the room, and I solemnly took three steps forward and bowed.

"King and Queen Firetail, it is a great honor to meet you," I greeted them.

I was about to introduce myself when the cloak let out the ultimate stinker. It was the most disgusting smell of all time — even worse than the stinkiest cheese at the All U Can Eat Cheese Palace! But no one realized the cloak had done it because he was INVISIBLE!

"Who made that stink?" the king thundered.

"Oh, what a **horrible** smell!" the queen shrieked, pinching her nostrils.

"It was the knight!" cawed the crow.

Not again! I didn't want to take the BLAME, but I had to. After all, I couldn't tell everyone that I had the Invisible Cloak with me.

"U-um, well, yes, i-it was me," I stammered, my fur turning as red as the ruby dragons around me. "Please eXCuSe me!"

"Instead of calling you the fearless knight they should call you the super-stinky knight!" one of the dragons teased me.

"The next time we fight with the dragons from the NeighborinG land, we'll put you on the front lines," said Redtooth, the dragon army general. "You'll KNOCK THEM all out!"

"That knight may be

Redtooth,
**dragon army
general**

𝒽𝒶𝓃𝒹𝓈𝑜𝓂𝑒, but he's terribly
𝕊𝕄𝔼𝕃𝕃𝕐!" I overheard
the queen's lady's maid
whisper to her neighbor.

How embarrassing!

Pinky Sharpclaws,
lady's maid

The king's doctor came right up
to me and stuck a spoonful of **castor oil** in my
mouth. **YUCK!**

"Drink this medicine right away, Knight!" he

Here!

Gulp!

Dr. Darkwing,
dragon doctor

insisted. "Your **terrible gas** will be gone in no time, you'll see!"

In response, the cloak let out three more stink bombs: TOOT! TOOT! TOOT!

"Ahhhh!" the dragons all shrieked.

"Enough, Knight!" King Firetail ordered. "We're suffocating. Try to control yourself, please."

"**CAWWW!**" Cleverwing squawked. "I tell him that all the time, but he doesn't listen to me."

If I could have plucked his feathers out **one** by **one**, I would have. Instead, I scolded the cloak under my whiskers.

Dragonbreath,
a page

"You're making a **terrible** first impression!" I whispered.

A page named Dragonbreath showed me to my **room**, which held a **RUBY** bed with **RUBY** sheets. **Ouch!** They weren't very comfortable!

And when I sat down to dinner, I realized the main course was . . . **RUBY SOUP**!

Ruby soup

I tried the soup, hoping for the best, but it was horrid. I went to bed on an empty stomach. Then I *tossed* and turned all night, shivering on that hard bed under those SHARP, cold ruby sheets. I tried moving closer to the fireplace, but even the fire was made of rubies! It wasn't warm at all.

Fireplace with a ruby fire

Unable to sleep, I tried to read a book. But every one I found was made of **RUBIES**. I couldn't even turn the pages.

Finally, after a very long, sleepless night, the sun began to rise outside my window.

Ruby book

THE SOLUTION IS
ON PAGE 311.

AN EXTREMELY RARE PEACOCK FEATHER

After an inedible ruby **breakfast**, Bloodtooth, a dragon guard, showed me to the room where the CRYSTAL SPHERE had been stored before it disappeared. A beautiful fountain stood in the middle of the room.

King Firetail was waiting for me there.

"This is the Guarding Fountain," he explained with **tears** in his eyes. "I placed the sphere here so no one would steal it. But someone managed to make the fountain fall asleep and **snatched** the sphere!"

I stepped closer to the fountain to look for clues. The fountain was **snoring** peacefully. There were **CHAMOMILE** flowers in the

Bloodtooth, dragon guard

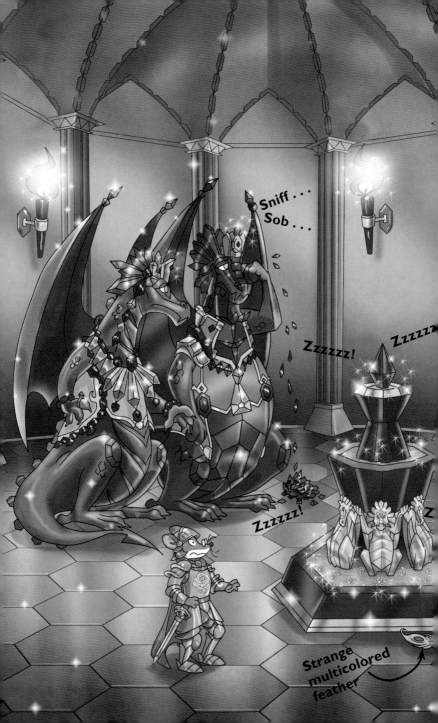

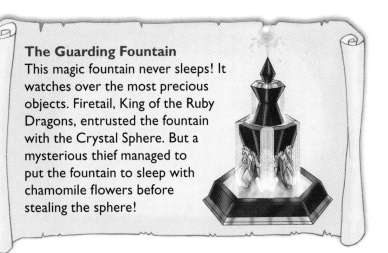

The Guarding Fountain
This magic fountain never sleeps! It watches over the most precious objects. Firetail, King of the Ruby Dragons, entrusted the fountain with the Crystal Sphere. But a mysterious thief managed to put the fountain to sleep with chamomile flowers before stealing the sphere!

tub — that's how the mysterious thief put the fountain to **SLEEP**! Then I noticed a strange **MULTICOLORED FEATHER** on the ground. I bent down to pick it up.

"Do you know whose feather this is?" I asked King Firetail.

The raven began leafing through a book entitled *Quills, Feathers, and Plumes of the Kingdom of Fantasy.* He pointed to a picture in the book.

"Here!" he cawed. "It's an extremely rare **peacock** feather."

I put the **feather** in my bag and thought about the strange **GOLD BUCKLE** from Blossom's study. Those were my only clues, and I had **no idea** what they meant! I sighed. Hopefully I would find more clues soon.

Hmmmm . . . let's see . . .

THE ART OF THE SCAM FROM A TO Z

Since I had completed my mission in the **EMPIRE OF RUBY DRAGONS**, it was time for me to leave.

"Thank you for your hospitality, Your Majesty," I told King Firetail.

"Can't you **stay** a while longer, Knight?" he replied.

But at that moment, the cloak let seven **stinkers** rip, each one bigger than the last!

Knight, please stay . . .

Toot!

FT!FF! PFFFFFT!FF! PFFFFFT!FF! PFFFFFT!FF! PFFFFFT!F

"If you have to go, we understand!" the king said quickly. "Good-bye! Have a nice trip!"

Then he picked me up and showed me to the DOOR.

Cleverwing, the Invisible Cloak, and I headed down the road. As soon as we were far enough away from the castle, the raven and I boarded the cloak again. Then we flew off into the sky.

As we flew, Cleverwing pumped me for career advice.

"Knight, I know you're an editor and a writer," he said slyly. "I want to write a book! I'm going to call it *The Art of the Scam from A to Z*. What do you think?"

"Well, it's not really my kind of book, but I'd be happy to take a look at it for you," I responded kindly. I didn't want him to be discouraged. Even scam artists can have dreams of being published authors!

Hearing this, the cloak became very jealous. In retaliation, he let out a stink bomb that really took my *breath* away.

When I asked him what was wrong, he told me

Cleverwing's Secret
He wants to write a book called *The Art of the Scam from A to Z*. Geronimo has promised to help him.

he wanted to write a book, too! It was going to be full of **silly jokes**. I had to promise to help him as well. What else could I do? I could only hope he didn't eat too many **beans** while we worked on it. **Poor me!**

I pulled out the map of the *Kingdom of Fantasy* to make sure we were heading toward the Kingdom of the Hissing Serpents. We had to find out more about what had happened to the WHISPERING WAND.

I saw on the map that we needed to head toward a pyramid-shape brown mountain.

"Keep going straight, Cloak!" I said. "We should be there in a few days."

"We need to be very **careful**," Cleverwing

The Invisible Cloak's Secret
He wants to write a book called *Silly Jokes to Make You Laugh*. Geronimo has promised to help him, too!

SiLLY JOKES

An invisible cloak was feeling very sick, so he went to the doctor.

"Wait here," the nurse told the cloak, and went to find the doctor.

"Doctor, there's an invisible cloak in your waiting room," the nurse told the doctor.

"Tell him I can't see him now," the doctor replied. "Next patient, please!"

Two **TROLLS** were at a restaurant. The first troll told his friend about a duel he had with a huge, scary dragon.

"Wow, what an adventure!" the friend said. "Your story leaves me breathless."

"That's great!" the first troll replied. "You just ate all that stinky onion and garlic soup, and I didn't want to smell your breath anyway!"

What flies through the air and stinks?

A smelly-copter!

added. "I've heard that those serpents really love fresh **MOUSE MEAT**. Maybe you could say you're something else, like an elephant. Or maybe a **CROCODILE**? Or an **anteater**? If they figure out you're a mouse, you're **fried**. I mean, they won't even wait to fry you — they'll eat you just as you are. And then how will I get my **GOLD**? Cawww!"

After three days and three **NIGHTS** of flying and listening to Cleverwing babble on and on while the cloak stunk up the entire sky, I was ready to land. Finally, I spotted the pyramid-shape mountain I had seen on the map.

"We've arrived at the Kingdom of the Hissing Serpents!" I squeaked.

THE KINGDOM OF THE HISSING SERPENTS

WHERE ARE THE HISSING SERPENTS?

The Invisible Cloak landed in front of the pyramid. I was thrilled to put my paws on firm land again. Flying with those two was rough! But when I looked around me, I was disappointed. I needed help finding the next clue, but there was no one else around.

IT WAS TOTALLY SILENT!

We were in the middle of an enormouse desert, and a BURNING-HOT wind was blowing in my snout. Then I noticed some Fantasian writing etched in the center of the pyramid. Can you translate it?*

* You can find the Fantasian Alphabet on page 310.

It read: Hissing Serpents. We were in the right place . . . but it was so desolate!

"Where are these serpents?" I wondered aloud.

"I know how to find them," Cleverwing said slyly. "But I'll tell you only if you sign this contract for one hundred gold coins!"

"What?!" I squeaked indignantly. "Don't I owe you enough gold already?" But I didn't have any other ideas, so I signed the paper.

"CAWWW!" the raven gloated happily. "You really are a FOOL! If I had met you earlier, I would be rich by now!"

Then he tapped the ground with one foot.

Sigh!

You really are a fool! Cawww!

"The entrance isn't **ABOVEGROUND** — it's belowground!" he said simply. Then he began to **scratch** the ground with his feet. "It's only for those who know how to find it. Ah, here it is! It's a secret passage, hidden under a rock. Let's go! CAWWW!"

He lifted a flat rock and a moment later DISAPPEARED underground. My whiskers trembling in fright, I followed him. The Invisible Cloak was close behind me.

The stairs were made of a strange substance that was smooth to the touch and very cold. We followed the raven DOWN, DOWN, DOWN. Toward the bottom of the steps, I saw a strange light and heard hypnotic flute and drum music.

HoLey cHeese! How cReepy!

The passageway ended in a cavernous room that had seven dark TUNNELS leading into it.

The Kingdom of the Hissing Serpents

1. ENTRANCE
2. COBRA TUNNEL
3. BLUE SERPENT TUNNEL
4. EMERALD SERPENT TUNNEL
5. WATER SERPENT TUNNEL
6. RATTLE SERPENT TUNNEL
7. ANACONDA TUNNEL
8. BOA SERPENT TUNNEL
9. SERPENT CAVE
10. ANACONDA SPRING
11. CORAL SERPENT PUDDLE
12. GREAT HISSING CAVERN

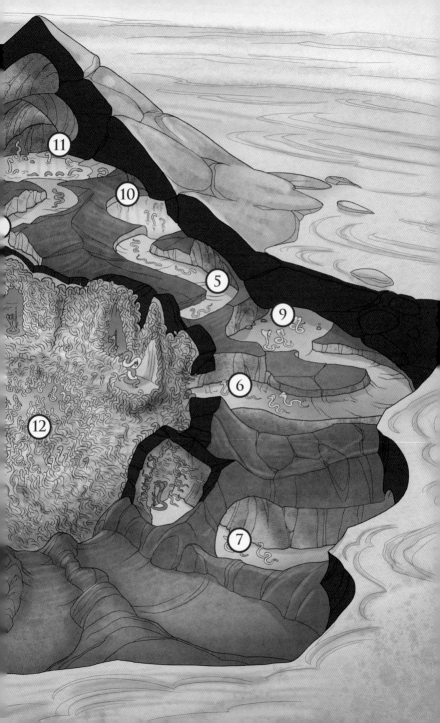

THE HISSING SERPENTS

The hissing serpents belong to the Slithering race and are of ancient and noble descent. They are very powerful because they know hypnosis and can read minds. Don't try to lie to a hissing serpent — he or she will know right away!

The hissing serpents are very dangerous because their venom is poisonous. But if you ask them kindly for help, they can also heal illnesses.

Their bodies are elastic: They can knot and weave themselves into shapes in order to build objects like tables, chairs, vases, and stairs. In fact, everything in their unsettling kingdom is made of live serpents!

They have forked tongues, so their speech sounds like hissing. And they always express themselves in rhyme so they can hypnotize whoever is listening!

THE POWER OF THE SERPENT'S EYE

At the center of the room there was a big fire that sparkled in the darkness, throwing flashes of light on the walls of the cavern.

Two serpents slithered up to me, staring at me with shining eyes.

"*Welcome to our kingdom, Knight,*" they hissed in unison. "*Look into our sssparkling light.*"

I APPROACHED them and bowed RESPECTFULLY.

"Nice to meet —"

But the two serpents interrupted before I could finish squeaking:

"*You don't even have to ssspeak;
There'sss no need for you to sssqueak.
We've already read your mind;
You can't hide thingsss from our kind!*"

Nice to meet —

Then all the serpents in the room began to chant in unison:

Look into the sssserpent'sss eye . . . do not try to tell a lie . . .
Look into the sssserpent'sss eye . . . do not try to tell a lie . . .
ook into the sssserpent'sss eye . . . do not try to tell a lie . . ."

Suddenly, I began to get very, very tired. I closed my eyes for a second, just to catch a little ratnap.

Luckily, someone (the Invisible Cloak!) pinched my right ear. **Ouchie!** Then **SOMEONE** else (Cleverwing!) **POKED** my left **ear** with his beak. **Double ouchie!**

Ouchie!

"Squeeaak!" I yelled, waking up immediately.

"Be careful, **Knight**!" Cleverwing hissed in my ear. "They were **hypnotizing**

Double ouchie!

you! If you don't stay awake, how will you find the three magical objects, save Queen Blossom, and, most important, pay me my gold coins?"

As much as I hated to admit it, that ANNOYING bird did have a point.

I turned to the two serpents again.

"I am Sir Geronimo of Stilton," I said confidently. "Who are you?"

The pair hissed a reply in unison:

"We are two ssserpentsss with a special bond. We are guardiansss of the Whispering Wand!"

"And where are all the other serpents?" I asked them.

The two **smiled** and replied:

"They're all around — sssee one, then more; They are the wallsss . . . they are the floor!"

I heard a strange swishing sound as I scanned

184

the room. Suddenly, I realized that everything around me — from the ground to the walls — was made of slithery serpents. Gulp!

The serpents all began to sing:

"Ancient and powerful are we!
Here's sssome ssserpent history:
We use our eyes to hypnotize,
Don't be sssurprised if you're mesmerized.
We think of only what'sss good and true,
Our mindsss are pure and our heartsss are, too.
We are ressspected both near and far,
All in the kingdom know who we are.
We are keepersss of the Whispering Wand,
Now that it'sss gone we will respond.
Thievesss and crooksss should all beware,
Cross the ssserpentsss if you dare!"

THE MYSTERIOUS THIEF

The raven cawed irritably.

"Okay, okay, we get it," Cleverwing squawked. "You guys are **powerful** and *mysterious*. So what? Someone still managed to nab the WHISPERING WAND when you were supposed to be watching it! So, who was the thief, huh? We're on a

Cawww!

Snap!

NEED-TO-KNOW basis, and we need to know! The sooner we find the thief and save Blossom, the sooner I can get my gold coins! **CAWWW!**"

The silver serpent darted forward, biting Cleverwing's tail feathers.

"**OUCH!**" Cleverwing squawked. Then he fell to the floor in a heap.

"Please, **HELP** my friend!" I begged.

The serpents replied:

*"Whoopsss — sssorry, we thought
your friend was food,
But that'sss what happensss when
you're mean and rude!"*

"He didn't mean to **offend** you," I begged. "Please save him! And if you can tell me who stole the WHISPERING WAND, that would be great, too! It's up to me to find the wand and save Queen Blossom."

Please save my friend!

The serpents were quiet for a minute.
Then they sang:

"Knight, you are a ssspecial guessst,
And we will help you with your quessst.
The magic wand must be disssscovered,
So Queen Blossom can be recovered.
For, without Her Majesssty,
The kingdom will be a travesssty!
We will tell you what we know:
The thief was quick to come and go.
But he left sssomething behind,
Sssome gray cat hair for you to find!"

The serpents showed me a strange tuft of CAT HAIR. The thief had left another MYSTERIOUS clue!

Next the serpents turned their attention to Cleverwing. They pried open the raven's mouth and poured a drop of FIRE-RED liquid in. It was the antidote to their poison!

As soon as the raven swallowed the liquid, he opened his eyes and flapped his wings.

Cawww!

"CAWWW!" he squawked.

Before he could say another thing, I grabbed his beak with my paw.

"That means 'thank you' in raven," I told the serpents. The last thing I needed was for Cleverwing to **INSULT** the snakes again!

We said good-bye to the serpents and **climbed** back up the vertical tunnel that led outside. There, we boarded the **Invisible Cloak** and took off into the **night**. This time, I didn't know where to go. I had three **STRANGE** clues, but no idea how to find the thief who had left them behind!

I still needed to figure out **who** the thief was, **WHERE** the thief was hiding, and **WHY** the thief had taken the three **magical** objects.

HERE ARE THE THREE
STRANGE CLUES WE FOUND . . .

A strange
gold buckle

A STRANGE,
RARE
PEACOCK
FEATHER

A STRANGE
TUFT OF CAT
HAIR

CATS IN BOOTS . . .
HOW SCARY!

We flew for a while through the **DARK** sky, unsure of where to go next. Before we knew it, a thick gray fog enveloped us.

"**CAWWW!**" the raven complained. "I can't even see past my beak!"

I hated to admit it, but we were **LOST**.

"Knight, I'm scared," the cloak whimpered softly. "I want to go home!"

Then a few rays of light from the moon filtered through the fog. I saw that we were in a hilly countryside covered in thick vegetation. Where were we? I didn't have a **CLUE**! But then I looked down. The fog parted briefly and a cavern appeared *BELOW* us.

"Let's spend the night there," Cleverwing

suggested. "It's too *dangerous* to travel at night."

"But that cavern looks *dangerous*, too," I replied. "What if someone *sneaks* in during the night and chops off my tail?"

My whiskers trembled with fright just thinking about it.

"CAWWW!" the raven replied. "Don't worry so much about your tail! We'll be fine."

"I want to stop, too, Knight," the cloak whispered. "I'm **tired** of flying. I need a rest."

So I reluctantly agreed to sleep in the cavern for the night. But I was so jumpy I couldn't fall asleep! Only at dawn did I finally drift off . . .

A short while later, Cleverwing woke me suddenly.

"CAWWW!" he whispered, pecking me on the ear. "Someone's coming!"

He pointed to two figures approaching the

We are Cats in Boots!

cavern along the path.

Cheese niblets! They were Cats in Boots!

One cat was tall and THiN and had three falcon feathers in his hat. The other was a CHUBBY gray cat with two peacock feathers in his cap. They were both wearing tall, colorful boots.

The cloak pointed to the gray cat.

"Look!" he whispered.

I studied the cat closely and realized only one of his boots had a shiny gold buckle. The other buckle was missing! And the feathers in his cap looked just like the strange, rare peacock feather that we found in the Empire of the Ruby Dragons!

Cats in Boots

The Cats in Boots are the slyest felines in the Kingdom of Fantasy. They live in the Land of Fairy Tales, but you can find them in any corner of the kingdom. They always wear tall, colorful boots and large hats with long feathers in them. They love to eat fish, but some adore fresh mouse meat, too.

Be careful around them: They often work for evil wizards or wicked witches!

Finally, the fur on his tail was the exact same color as the tuft of gray fur that we found in the Kingdom of the Hissing Serpents!

FIRST CLUE

"That's the thief we're after!" I gasped.

The **CATS** began chattering to each other.

SECOND CLUE

"**SHHH!**" I told Cleverwing and the cloak. "Let's be quiet and listen."

"Did you hear that the three most **POWERFUL** magical objects in the kingdom were stolen?" the gray cat was boasting.

THIRD CLUE

"I know WHO stole them, **WHY** they were stolen, and *where* they were taken!"

"Wow!" the other cat meoWeD in admiration.

Shhh! Let's listen!

"You're one brave and courageous cat!"

"Cawww!" the raven said softly. "We need to follow them right away!"

SLOWLY HEADING WEST

The **CHUBBY** gray cat said good-bye to his friend and headed west. We followed him closely — but not too closely! We didn't want to be discovered, but we didn't want to lose him, either. I was TERRIFIED that the cat would notice us.

We traveled for three days, slowly heading west. Every once in a while I would check the map, but I couldn't seem to figure out what our destination was. Sometimes the cat stopped and sniffed the air suspiciously, as if he smelled a rat.

Yikes! I kept the Invisible Cloak close by just in case I had to HIDE.

On the third day, disaster struck. The cat began to look over his shoulder constantly.

HE TOOK A FEW STEPS AND ... ZIP! HE TURNED!

HE WENT A LITTLE FARTHER AND ... ZAP! HE TURNED!

HE TOOK A FEW MORE STEPS AND ... ZOP! HE TURNED!

Each time, Cleverwing and I hid under the cloak. But the raven always pulled him **ONE WAY** and I pulled the **OTHER WAY**. It was a constant **BACK** and **FORTH**!

What would we do if the cat saw us? **Squeak!**

After a lot of tug-of-war with the cloak, we reached a sign written in Fantasian. Can you translate it?*

*You can find the Fantasian Alphabet on page 310.

It read BEWARE: FLYING FLEAS.

Only then did I **understand** the cat's STRANGE behavior. He didn't smell a mouse . . . he was looking out for fleas!

And at that moment, the fleas **ATTACKED** us. **CRUSTY KITTY LITTER!** Those fleas were itchier than the wool socks my aunt Ratilda knit for my birthday last year. I couldn't stop scratching!

I scratched, and scratched, and scratched as we walked, and walked, and walked.

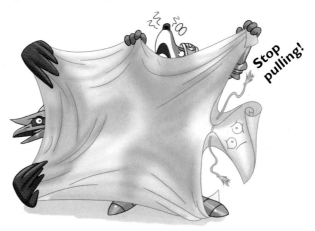

Stop pulling!

As we continued west, we all became more TIRED, sad, and downcast than we had ever been before. I thought mournfully of my cozy kitchen at home with its *FULLY STOCKED* fridge. When would I ever return?

"Cawww!" the raven protested. "It's always so **depressing** to walk west, especially when you get too close to the LAND OF A THOUSAND SHADOWS."

I grabbed the **map** and realized that's right where we were headed! At **sunset** on the seventh day, we entered a valley surrounded by tall, CRAGGY mountains. Behind them, the setting sun cast long, dark shadows over everything.

We had arrived in the GLOOMY Land of a Thousand Shadows!

THE LAND OF A THOUSAND SHADOWS

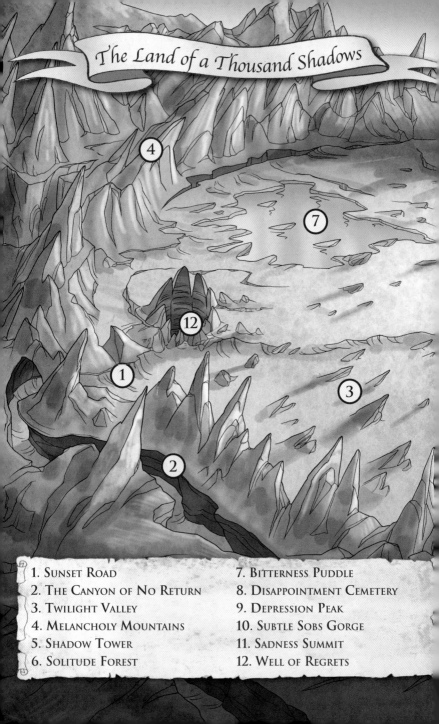

The Land of a Thousand Shadows

1. Sunset Road
2. The Canyon of No Return
3. Twilight Valley
4. Melancholy Mountains
5. Shadow Tower
6. Solitude Forest
7. Bitterness Puddle
8. Disappointment Cemetery
9. Depression Peak
10. Subtle Sobs Gorge
11. Sadness Summit
12. Well of Regrets

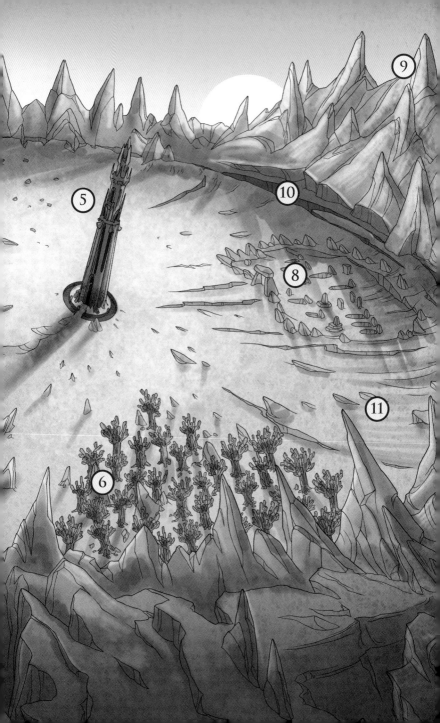

WANTED: WIZARD'S APPRENTICE

After just a short time there, I realized that the sun never rises or sets in the Land of a Thousand Shadows. It **ALWAYS** remains in the same position in the sky, casting the LONGEST, **DARKEST** shadows all day long. HOW GLOOMY!

The raven pointed to a building in the center of the valley.

"Do you see that really TALL tower, Knight?" he asked. "It's Shadow Tower, home of the wizard

What a sad place!

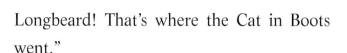

Longbeard! That's where the Cat in Boots went."

Just looking at that ominous tower gave me GOOSE BUMPS under my fur.

As we slowly approached, I realized the building was made entirely of shadows.

HoLey cHeese! What a terrible place! It was built with SHADOW bricks and SHADOW cement. It had SHADOW roofs, SHADOW doors, and SHADOW windows. Even the doormat in front of the door and the doorbell were SHADOWS!

A SHADOW SIGN hung from the SHADOW DOOR.

WANTED:
WIZARD'S APPRENTICE

P.S. DON'T WASTE MY TIME OR I'LL
MAKE YOU VANISH INTO THIN AIR!

SIGNED, LONGBEARD THE WIZARD

"Here's our way in, Knight," Cleverwing said slyly. "Pretend you're applying for the position as the **wizard's apprentice**!

I've got just the things you'll need."

He rummaged through his chest and pulled out a cat costume.

"It's yours for just **thirty gold coins**!" he said.

Argh!

① I put on a fake-cat-fur costume.

Ouch!

② The raven sewed on a cat tail.

"No way!" I squeaked. "I'm not paying you another cent!"

But the raven was already rubbing me with a sponge soaked in **Feline Fur Cologne**. It smelled just like **FEAR** . . . uh, I mean **CAT**!

"This will cover up your mousy smell," he explained. **"CAWWW!"**

Then he made me put on the **fake-fur** suit and a **cat tail**. He glued long whiskers and pointy cat ears on me and gave me a **GREEN**

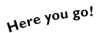

Here you go!

What a classy cat!

③

He glued on long cat whiskers.

④

Then he gave me a velvet jacket.

velvet jacket with **GOLD** buttons.

But he wasn't done yet! Next he gave me a pair of **BOOTS**, a large hat with a **feather** in it, and a **SILVER** sword to hang from my belt. Finally, he pulled out a mirror.

"**CAWWW!** Take a look!" he said. "Am I the best scam artist or what? Your own grandmother wouldn't even **RECOGNIZE** you!"

How do I get these on?

Here's the finishing touch!

5 Next was a pair of boots, and a hat with a feather in it.

6 Then he gave me a silver sword!

I took one look in the mirror and yelped in fright. I really did look like a **cat**! Cleverwing handed me a smoked-salmon pie and pushed me toward the door to Shadow Tower. He and the cloak stayed behind.

"Tell the cat you're from the Land of Fairy Tales, too," the raven advised. "Then offer him the salmon pie. He'll treat you well!"

Yikes!

Now go!

Okay!

⑦ I looked in the mirror . . . Squeak! How scary!

⑧ I was ready to see the wizard!

A Pie for Fluffy

I knocked on the door with a **trembling** paw.

"Meow! Who's there?" answered a gruff voice.

I had been SCARED before, but now I was REALLY, REALLY terrified!

"Umm, I'm a C-C-Cat in Boots from the Land of Fairy Tales," I replied, trying my best to imitate the cat's **scary** voice.

The door to Shadow Tower burst open to reveal the gray cat we had followed. The cat was **wider** than he was tall — he was as **round** as a giant wheel of cheese. He had a CHUBBY face, CHUBBY ears, and a CHUBBY belly. Even his whiskers were CHUBBY!

He was wearing a red velvet jacket that was covered in GREASY stains from different

FLUFFY DE WHISKERPUSS

who he is: A big gray cat and a member of the De Whiskerpuss family. He's been great at picking locks ever since he was a kitten, so his entire family calls him Picky!

what he does: He is the wizard Longbeard's assistant. He lives with him in the Land of a Thousand Shadows.

personality: He loves to brag and boast about his accomplishments. He's also very vain and deceitful.

his weakness: He puffs up his fur and acts brave around anyone smaller than him, but he becomes as tame as a little kitten whenever Longbeard is around.

his secret: He's terrified of his boss. He's also very proud of his collection of colorful boots.

his favorite food: Pretty much anything! He loves to eat.

A Pie for Fluffy

kinds of food: tuna sauce (I could tell by a fishbone), a cherry pie (I could tell by the crumbs), and cheddar cheese sauce (I could tell by the smell).

"I am Fluffy De Whiskerpuss," he growled **MENACINGLY**. "Who are you?

"Umm, I w-was . . . I mean, I would be . . . I m-mean, I'm one of your k-kind!" I stuttered. "See my boots? And I brought you this salmon pie as a gift. Umm, I would like to apply for the job as the WIZARD'S APPRENTICE!"

The cat broke into a grin.

"Welcome, feline friend," he meowed, patting me on the back. "Come on in! It's so nice to see another furry feline face! Around here it's always just SHADOWS, SHADOWS, and more SHADOWS!"

Then he grabbed the pie, cut a big piece, and shoved it into his mouth.

"Mmmm . . . yummy!" he meowed. "I just adore smoked-salmon pie!"

He suddenly sniffed the air SUSPICIOUSLY.

"Hey, do you smeLL something funny?" he asked. "Something . . . mousy?"

"Um, no, I don't smell a thing!" I squeaked.

"Hmmm . . . strange," he muttered. "Hey, good PIE, by the way! They don't make them like that around these

WANTED:
WIZARD'S APPRENTICE

P.S. DON'T WASTE MY TIME OR I'LL
MAKE YOU VANISH INTO THIN AIR!
SIGNED, LONGBEARD THE WIZARD

Wow . . . you're hungry!

Yum!

parts. Everything here is just made of shadows, and those aren't very **tasty** or **filling**!"

"Glad you liked it," I replied quickly. "So, about that wizard's apprentice job . . ."

"Of course I'll put in a **GOOD WORD** for you, feline friend!" he meowed.

"Thanks!" I replied. "I really am a **LUCKY** mou — I mean, **CAT**! So, um, what exactly is the job description?"

"The job begins at seven a.m. **SHARP** every day," he explained. "You'll be busy until five p.m. every night, and the pay is three gold florins a month. Lodging and meals are included, but it's always **SHADOW** food. Blech!"

He sniffed the air **SUSPICIOUSLY** a second time.

"Are you sure you don't smell that?" he asked. "It definitely smells like a **plump**, **juicy** mouse!"

"No, no, no," I replied. "I don't smell a thing!

"Hmmm . . . **very strange**," he muttered. "Anyway I'll introduce you to **LONGBEARD**. And I'll say some good things about you. After all, we cats have to stick together, right?"

"Right!" I agreed in my *gruff*, fake cat voice. "S-so wh-what's Longbeard like?"

Fluffy burst out laughing.

"Hee, hee, hee! Meow!" He giggled. "He's very strange. He's **DANGEROUS** and **POWERFUL**, but he has a lot of hang-ups. For example, he's **OBSESSED** with gold. He wants as much gold as possible. Sometimes he even uses his magic to try to *create* it! But mostly he's obsessed with **secrecy**, so I really shouldn't tell you any more!"

"Couldn't you tell me just a **teeny, tiny** bit more?" I asked. "After all, we cats have to stick together, right?"

That seemed to work, because he **SPILLED THE BEANS** right away.

"Well, okay, I'll tell you a little more about the wizard . . . and about me!" he whispered proudly. "I'm such a *clever* cat that I just helped him steal three of the most **POWERFUL** magical objects in the entire Kingdom of Fantasy. He's

We cats have to stick together!

Um . . . of course!

hiding them here in Shadow Tower. And that's not all, but I definitely can't tell you the rest!"

I SHUDDERED WITH FEAR.

Holey cheese, what a terrible place this was! And my only friend was a cat, of all creatures!

JUST THE THOUHT MADE ME FEEL FAINT

LONGBEARD THE WIZARD

He is a descendent of the Dynasty of the Darkest Wizards. His father was the famous **wizard Deceptimus**, King of Deceptive Illusions. His mother was the illustrious **sorceress Morganica**, also known as the Princess of Fleeting Dreams.

No one knows his real name, but because he has a long, dark beard, everyone calls him **Longbeard**.

Longbeard is the most mysterious wizard in the Kingdom of Fantasy. He lives in the most mysterious land, the Land of a Thousand Shadows, in the most mysterious place, **SHADOW TOWER**.

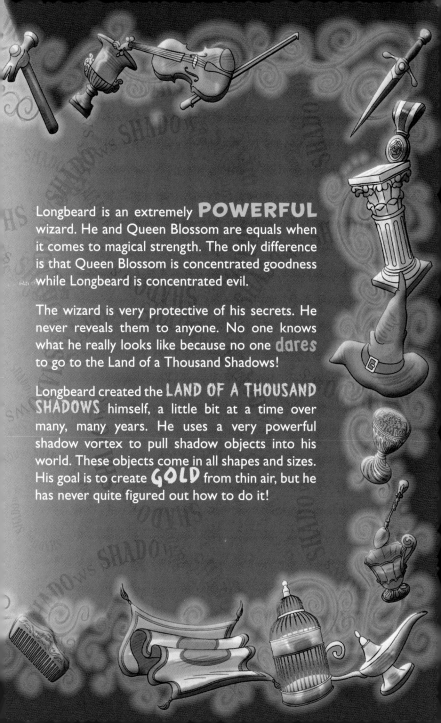

Longbeard is an extremely **POWERFUL** wizard. He and Queen Blossom are equals when it comes to magical strength. The only difference is that Queen Blossom is concentrated goodness while Longbeard is concentrated evil.

The wizard is very protective of his secrets. He never reveals them to anyone. No one knows what he really looks like because no one **dares** to go to the Land of a Thousand Shadows!

Longbeard created the **LAND OF A THOUSAND SHADOWS** himself, a little bit at a time over many, many years. He uses a very powerful shadow vortex to pull shadow objects into his world. These objects come in all shapes and sizes. His goal is to create **GOLD** from thin air, but he has never quite figured out how to do it!

THE SHADOW VORTEX

Fluffy sniffed the air **suspiciously** yet again.

"Are you positive you don't smell that?" he asked. "I'm absolutely certain there's a delicious mouse around here somewhere!"

"I don't smell a thing!" I replied again.

At that moment, the bell above Fluffy's head rang: Ding! Ding! Diiiiiiiing!

A booming voice **THUNDERED** from a brass loudspeaker hanging on the wall:

"Fluffy, where are you? Come here at once, you flea-ridden cat!"

"Yes, LONGBEARD," Fluffy meowed back nervously. "I'll be right there, Sir Wizard!"

Then he grabbed my tail and DRAGGED me with him.

"Follow me, feline friend!" he meowed.

"You're about to meet the mysterious wizard Longbeard!"

"Okay, I'll follow you," I replied as he yanked my tail. "Meowww!"

Fluffy dragged me down a SHADOWY hallway, through several SHADOWY rooms, and up a SHADOWY flight of stairs. That Shadow Tower is such a SPOOKY place!

1. SHADOWY ENTRANCE
2. ROOM OF THE DANCING
   SHADOWS
3. SHADOWY RECEPTION ROOM
4. SHADOWY LIBRARY
5. SHADOWY THRONE ROOM
6. LABORATORY OF WIZARD SECRETS
7. SHADOWY ROOMS
8. SHADOW VORTEX ROOM
9. MYSTERIOUS ROOM (NO ONE
   KNOWS WHAT'S IN THERE!)
10. SUPER-SHADOWY BASEMENT

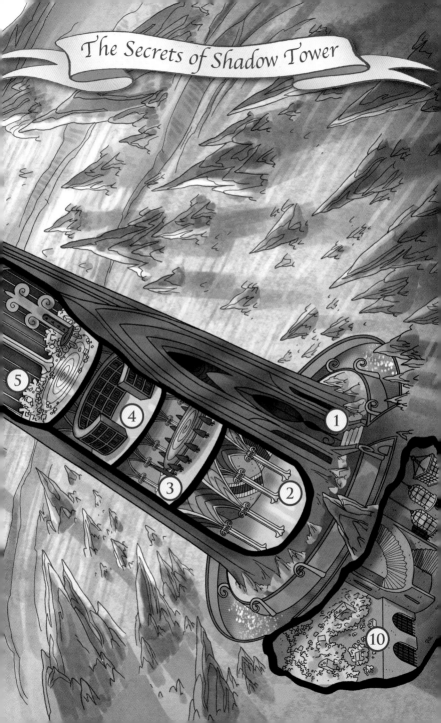

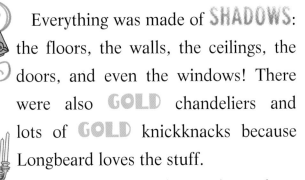

Everything was made of SHADOWS: the floors, the walls, the ceilings, the doors, and even the windows! There were also GOLD chandeliers and lots of GOLD knickknacks because Longbeard loves the stuff.

The most extraordinary thing about all the shadowy objects was that they came in so many different shades of shadow, from deep black to light gray. Can you imagine a place where you eat on a shadow table, with GOLD and SHADOW plates, GOLD and SHADOW glasses, and GOLD and SHADOW utensils?

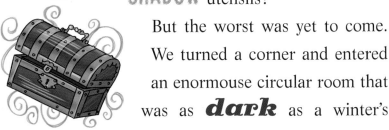

But the worst was yet to come. We turned a corner and entered an enormouse circular room that was as *dark* as a winter's night, and very windy. It seemed like we were in the middle of a tornado!

My whiskers trembled with fear.

SQUEAK! HOW SCARY!

A strange character stood at the center of the VORTEX. I couldn't get a good look at him because his back was to me. He was reading from a mysterious book and muttering what sounded like magic spells as he extended his arms toward the vortex.

At each word, the vortex spit out an item made of SHADOWS!

"SHADOWS, SHADOWS, and more SHADOWS!" he shouted, frustrated. "Why can't I create GOLD?"

The wizard pulled out everyday objects like glasses, books, and shoelaces, as well as PRECIOUS objects like necklaces, earrings, and

crowns. But nothing was made of **GOLD**.

"Check it out!" Fluffy whispered to me proudly. "Longbeard is such a powerful wizard, he can use the **SHADOW VORTEX** to create anything . . . well, almost anything! He hasn't quite figured out how to make **GOLD** objects, and that makes him really, really **ANGRY**!"

The wizard turned toward us, and I got a better look at him. He was tall and **BONY** with eyes as black as carbon and as piercing as nails.

Another shadow? I want gold, gold, gooooold!

He was wearing a tall, pointed hat and a long **MIDNIGHT-BLUE** robe that went down to his feet. It was dotted with golden stars that *sparkled* in the semidarkness.

He had a thick *curly* black beard that had grown very long, way past his feet! But his most striking feature was the bright gold ring that he wore on the pinky finger of his left hand. It was shaped like a **VORTEX**.

Fluffy whispered to me that it was the **magic ring** the wizard used to perform his shadowy spells!

The magic ring

I'll Turn You Into a Warty Toad!

Fluffy bowed down until his WHISKERS grazed the ground.

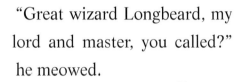
My master...

"Great wizard Longbeard, my lord and master, you called?" he meowed.

"It's about time!" WIZARD LONGBEARD snarled. "Next time, you'd better run when the bell rings. Got it? Otherwise I'll turn you into a Warty toad!"

"Yes, boss," Fluffy replied meekly.

Then Longbeard noticed me.

Thundering cat tails! He did NOT look happy to see me.

"And WHO are you?" he roared. "Don't LIE

to me, because I'll know!"

"Umm, h-hello, Y-Your M-Majesty," I stammered, trembling. "Er, I mean Mister Wizard. I am hoping to become your NEW APPRENTICE."

"Boss, this is a buddy of mine," Fluffy quickly explained. "He's a Cat in Boots, just like me! He's a trustworthy feline — I just KNOW it!"

"A Cat in Boots, you say?" the wizard huffed. "And yet my wizardly instinct tells me there is something strange about this little kitty."

He stared at me with his PIERCING eyes. I thought I might faint! Then he sniffed the air.

Jokes About Toads

Q: What is a toad's favorite flower?
A: A CROAKUS!

Q: What goes "dot-dot-croak, dot-dash-croak"?
A: MORSE TOAD!

"Hey, Fluffernutter," he asked Fluffy. "Do you smell something **mousy** in the air?"

"Of course I do!" the cat **MEOWED** loudly. "I've been smelling it for a while now!"

"I d-don't smell a thing!" I denied it meekly for the fourth time.

Luckily, at that moment the SHADOW VORTEX began to buzz and Longbeard went back to his wicked work.

"I've already wasted too much **time**," he said. Then he pointed at me. "You! Sign the contract! The WIZARD'S APPRENTICE job is yours."

WORK CONTRACT

Wizard's Apprentice

I promise:

- NOT TO OPEN THE CLOSETS!
- NOT TO RUMMAGE THROUGH DRAWERS!
- NOT TO SPY THROUGH KEYHOLES!
- NOT TO PERFORM UNAUTHORIZED SPELLS!
- NOT TO MOVE BOOKS FROM THE BOOKSHELVES!
- NOT TO TOUCH ANYTHING EXCEPT TO CLEAN, DUST, OR POLISH IT!
- NOT TO TAKE NAPS DURING WORK HOURS!
- NOT TO PUT MY FINGERS IN MY NOSE!
- NOT TO BLAB ANY OF LONGBEARD'S SECRETS!

In exchange, I will receive three gold florins a month.

Signed,

The wizard strode toward a SHADOWY door with a SHADOWY sign:

LONGBEARD'S WIZARD LABORATORY
WOE TO THOSE WHO ENTER
WITHOUT PERMISSION!
(YOU JUST MIGHT VANISH INTO THIN AIR!)

Fluffy pushed me after him. We went through the door and entered a dark room with bookshelves full of **magic** books, shelves **LOADED** down with **magic** objects, and tables covered in **magic** tools. Basically, even a mouse like me who doesn't know much about **magic** could tell that this was a WIZARD'S laboratory.

"Here you go, fellow feline," Fluffy purred, clapping me on the back with his huge paw. (It had very **SHARP** claws!) "It's your first day as the WIZARD'S APPRENTICE, so do a good job. Remember, the Cats in Boots have a **reputation** to uphold!"

"Yes, yes, of course," I muttered. "Uh, long live the Cats in Boots! Now, um, what do I do, exactly?"

"Oh, LONGBEARD will explain everything," Fluffy replied with a chuckle. "Remember: If he's happy with you, he'll give you three GOLD FLORINS. But be careful! If he doesn't like your work: POOF! You'll **vanish** into thin air!"

A Mysterious
Silver Key

The wizard showed me around the laboratory.
Then he began to fire **orders** at me rapidly.

"Clean those **DIRTY** beakers!" he snarled.
"Then **sweep** the floor, dust the shelves, and **scrub** the cauldron!"

"Yes, master," I replied meekly.

"But be careful," he warned threateningly. "If I catch you opening the closets, SPYING through keyholes, RUMMAGING in my drawers, eavesdropping behind doors, performing unauthorized spells, EATING when it isn't mealtime, MOVING my books, SLEEPING on the job, using the same rag to CLEAN the bathroom and the plates, or blowing your nose on the curtains . . . I'll make you vanish into thin air!"

"Don't worry, Your Excellency," Fluffy said. "My friend here won't do any of those things."

"So you'll vouch for him?" the wizard grumbled.

"Oh, no way!" Fluffy replied with a chuckle. "I barely know this cat. I just said it because he seems okay to me."

WHAT? So much for Cats in Boots sticking together!

"D-don't worry," I stammered. "I won't blow my nose on the curtains. I'll definitely use a tissue!"

Longbeard didn't seem convinced, but he gave in in the end. He handed me a LARGE ring of keys.

"These are all the keys to Shadow Tower," he said. "I want you to clean it from TOP to bottom."

Then he pointed to a mysterious silver key shaped like a little vortex.

"Whatever you do, DON'T use this key," the

wizard warned. "If you do, I'll make you vanish into thin air!"

"Yeah, don't use that key!" Fluffy repeated. "**Meow!**"

I looked at the LITTLE SILVER KEY with curiosity. What did it open?

As soon as Fluffy and the wizard left me to

Don't use this key!

do my work, I began **LOOKING** around the room for clues. I was certain the three magical objects were hidden somewhere inside the Shadow Tower. But where were they? I had to find them before it was **too late**!

Then I got an IDEA. Maybe the little silver key was the answer. The wizard told me not to touch it, which meant it was probably **IMPORTANT**! My whiskers trembled as I though of what might happen to me if the wizard found out what I was doing. But the **MISSION** was too important — I had to gather my **COURAGE** and go for it!

So I *RAN* down the hallways, trying the key in all the locks. It didn't fit in

Where could they be?

any of them! In the end, there was just one
tiny door left. It was made from solid **silver**
and there was a SHADOW VORTEX carved on
the door.

I put the key in the **LOCK** and turned it. The
door opened with a creak.

Inside, there was a large trunk, a **ball** covered
by a black velvet cloth, and a long, slender wooden
case.

What a tiny door!

The Book of a
Thousand Spells

The Crystal Sphere

The Whispering Wand

Could they be the three objects I was looking for?

First I opened the trunk. There was a **BOOK** inside! I picked it up and a cloud of fairy glitter enveloped me. Sparkly letters on the book's cover read: The Book of a Thousand Spells!

Next I **LIFTED** the black velvet cloth and a shiny, transparent globe sparkled before me. It was the CRYSTAL SPHERE!

Finally, I opened the slender **WOODEN** case. It was the legendary WHISPERING WAND!

Fabumouse!

I had actually found the THREE MAGICAL OBJECTS! I couldn't believe my good fortune.

Suddenly, I began to feel very proud of myself. I was a hero! I began to fantasize about my return to Crystal Castle. The inhabitants of the Kingdom of Fantasy would be so thankful, surely they would build a **statue** in my honor. Or maybe they would name a street after me! Sometimes I doubted myself, but I really was a courageous, bold, and *fearless knight*!

I'm a hero!

But at that moment, I felt **something** pull at my jacket . . .

It was the Invisible Cloak! He had entered Shadow Tower secretly and tracked me down. He tugged at my sleeve again.

"What are you doing?" he whimpered. "Be careful!"

But I wasn't listening. I was feeling **TOO GOOD** about myself!

I had more important things to do than to listen to that **STINKY** Invisible Cloak! I had just completed my mission, and I had every right to **celebrate**.

Be careful!

Everything's fine!

Then I began to have **STRANGE** ideas. Maybe I could learn to use those three magical objects myself! I would become a wizard, and I would use my **powers** to find and free Queen Blossom!

There was only one thing to do: I put on Longbeard's spare cloak and hat . . .

HERE'S HOW I TRANSFORMED INTO A WIZARD!

1. I took off my cat costume . . .

2. I was in my cheese underwear!

3. I found Longbeard's spare clothes in a closet . . .

THE BOOK OF A THOUSAND SPELLS

I felt like a real wizard! I felt strong and **SUPER-POWERFUL**!

"I will free Queen Blossom!" I shouted boldly and confidently.

Then I opened The Book of a Thousand Spells and began to leaf through it. *There's nothing to it*, I thought. *I just need to find the right spell and wave the magic wand. It will be really easy!*

The Invisible Cloak began to jump around nervously, trying to *stop me*.

Stop!

If you are reading this
book, you should know
that this is . . .

The Book of a Thousand Spells!

This is the tool that was used to create
Crystal Castle at the beginning of time!

This is the most powerful book in
the Kingdom of Fantasy. Whoever
possesses it can create reality!

It was printed with magical ink that
appears and disappears and can be
seen only by those who are worthy!

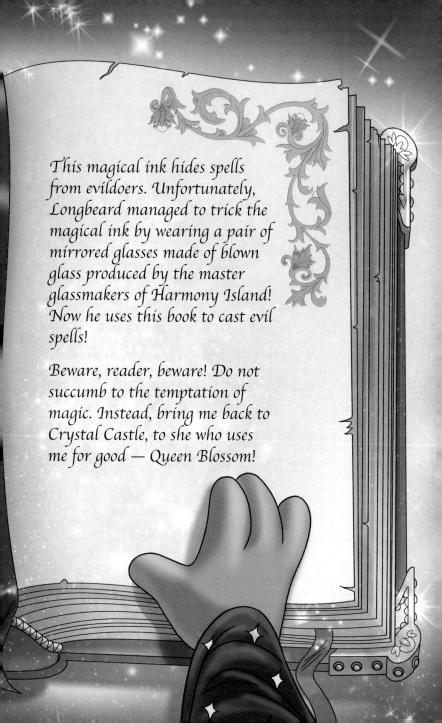

This magical ink hides spells from evildoers. Unfortunately, Longbeard managed to trick the magical ink by wearing a pair of mirrored glasses made of blown glass produced by the master glassmakers of Harmony Island! Now he uses this book to cast evil spells!

Beware, reader, beware! Do not succumb to the temptation of magic. Instead, bring me back to Crystal Castle, to she who uses me for good — Queen Blossom!

THE CRYSTAL SPHERE

The Book of a Thousand Spells warned me to be careful, but I didn't pay attention. I closed the book and turned to the CRYSTAL SPHERE. If I learned how to use the second magical object, I would be an even more **POWERFUL** wizard!

I put my hands on the CRYSTAL SPHERE. Inside the globe, many cloudy figures appeared.

When the cloak realized I was looking in the sphere, he **THREW** himself over it. He was trying to hide it so it would be invisible to me! The cloak managed to make the sphere DISAPPEAR. When I realized what he had done, I quickly **YANKED** him away.

"Get out of the way, Cloak!" I shouted.

"Stop, Knight!" he replied. "I beg you: Please StOP! Don't you see what's happening?"

You're just jealous of my powers!

The sphere is mine!

"You're just JEALOUS of my powers!" I yelled. "Do you want to become a wizard, too? You'll never be anything more than an invisible cloak. I, on the other hand, am Geronimo — the great, the magnificent, the all-powerful wizard! The CRYSTAL SPHERE is mine — all mine! — and no one can take it away. I will defend it even if it means losing my fur!"

I grabbed the sphere and held it close to me.

"It's my **precious treasure**!" I shouted loudly.

The Invisible Cloak began to **SOB** invisible tears. But I only had eyes for the **THREE MAGICAL OBJECTS**. I turned to the last object: the legendary WHISPERING WAND.

Don't you see what's happening?

Go away!

It's my treasure!

Sob!

THE WHISPERING
WAND

I reached out and tried to grab the WHISPERING
WAND, but it began to move! It rolled here
and there and BOUNCED around, refusing to
STAY STILL for me to catch it.

"Wand, I order you to come here!" I shouted.
"Obey the mighty and powerful wizard
Geronimo!"

Wand, come here!

In response, the wand SKITTERED even farther away from me!

I ran after it.

"Oh yeah?" I yelled. "I'm smarter than you, silly wand. I'll find a really powerful spell in The Book of a Thousand Spells and then you'll have to obey me!"

I flipped through the **BOOK** until I found the correct spell.

If you are re___ this book, you s___ ___now that this ___

The Book of ___housand Spells!

This is ti___ ___ that was used to create Crystal ___ ___ at the beginning of time! This ___ ___ ___ most powerful book in the ___ ___om of Fantasy. Whoever pos___ ___ can create reality! ___printed with magical ink that ___rs and disappears and can be ___ only by those who are worthy!

This magical ink hides spells from evildoers. Unfortunately, Longbeard managed to trick the magical ink by wearing a pair of mirrored glasses made of blown glass produced by the master glassmakers of Harmony Island! Now he uses this book to cast evil spells!

Beware, reader, beware! Do not succumb to the temptation of magic. Instead, bring me back to Crystal Castle, to she who uses me for good — Queen Blossom!

"*Whispering Wand in my hand,*" I chanted. "*Your every wish is my command!*"

The wand began to hit me over the head.

Smack!

Ouch!

Smack!

Smack!

I quickly realized my mistake: I had said the spell **incorrectly**! I guess the wand's wish was to hurt me, and it was coming true. **Ouch!**

I quickly corrected myself.

"*Whispering Wand in my hand,* MY *every wish is* YOUR *command!*" I shouted.

And then . . . the wand was in my **POWER**!

A REAL WIZARD . . . OR NOT?

The Invisible Cloak hid in a corner looking scared as I flipped through The Book of a Thousand Spells. I didn't understand what his **problem** was. He should have been so **proud** of me. After all, I was a **POWERFUL** wizard now!

The book was full of magic spells. There were spells to *travel* through time, spells to make things DISAPPEAR, and spells to make things reappear. There were *funny* spells that could make rocks laugh, and **SERIOUS** spells that could make a tree cry.

I chose a simple spell to practice my new powers. I would make a **TOAD** appear. The book said to WAVE the wand, but it didn't say for how long.

I decided to wave the wand for as long as it took for the toad to appear. Then I read the spell and chanted the words aloud:

*"Jump over there, jump over here,
Little toad, now you will appear!"*

I waved the wand once . . . twice . . . three times . . . four times . . . until a toad finally **APPEARED**!

I was feeling really **good** about myself. I had gone from a simple mouse to a **REAL** wizard

Jump over there . . .

Jump over here . . .

Ribbit!

in just **one** day! I figured I really was special. After all, I had been chosen to find Queen Blossom, right?

Moldy mozzarella! I had forgotten all about my mission to save Blossom! As soon as I found the magical objects, I had forgotten **everything** else!

Now that I remembered, it was time for me to do the **RIGHT THING**.

I turned toward the door and jumped back, startled.

Ribbit! Ribbit! Ribbit!

There were now **three** toads instead of **ONE**! And a moment later, there were **NINE TOADS**!

Ribbit . . . .

The toads kept multiplying!

What had I done wrong?

I glanced back at the book and saw a note in tiny print at the bottom of the page:

Ribbit . . . .

Important: Do not wave the wand more than three times! If you do, you will end up with ONE THOUSAND TOADS instead of one!

Holey cheese! What a **MESS**!

Ribbit . . . .

I searched the book frantically for a spell that would fix the problem, but I couldn't concentrate because the toads were croaking so loudly! Plus, the room was so DARK I was having trouble reading. I needed some light. I figured I'd try another spell.

Ribbit, Ribbit, Ribbit . . . . Ribbit, ribbit, ribbit . . . . Ribbit . . . . Ribbit, Ribbit, Ribbit . . . . Ribbit . . . .

How many
toads are in the
room so far?

"One candle is all I need, for this new spell to succeed," I chanted.

A moment later a candle **appeared** in front of me. But a second later, the candle set FIRE to the carpet, the curtains, and the furniture. In less than a minute, there were flames all around me!

Heeelp!

I frantically read a spell to put out the fire:

"Water, water, where are you?
Sprinkle down a drop or two!"

An enormouse gush of water poured over me. So much for a drop or two! At least the FIRE went out immediately.

I breathed a sign of relief. **PHEW!**

WATER, WATER, WHERE ARE YOU? SPRINKLE DOWN A DROP OR TWO!

WHAT A MESS!

Unfortunately, my relief was short lived. The waterfall didn't **stop**! Water continued to pour into the small room. Soon all the objects in the room were soaked — including the book!

I leafed through it frantically until I found a spell to stop the waterfall:

"Water, water, time to stop,
I don't need another drop!"

The waterfall disappeared, but the floor was covered in puddles. The toads splashed around happily, but I was miserable. What a mess! I had to clean it up quickly, before Longbeard found me and saw what I had done!

I finally understood what had happened: The magical objects had ENCHANTED me, and I

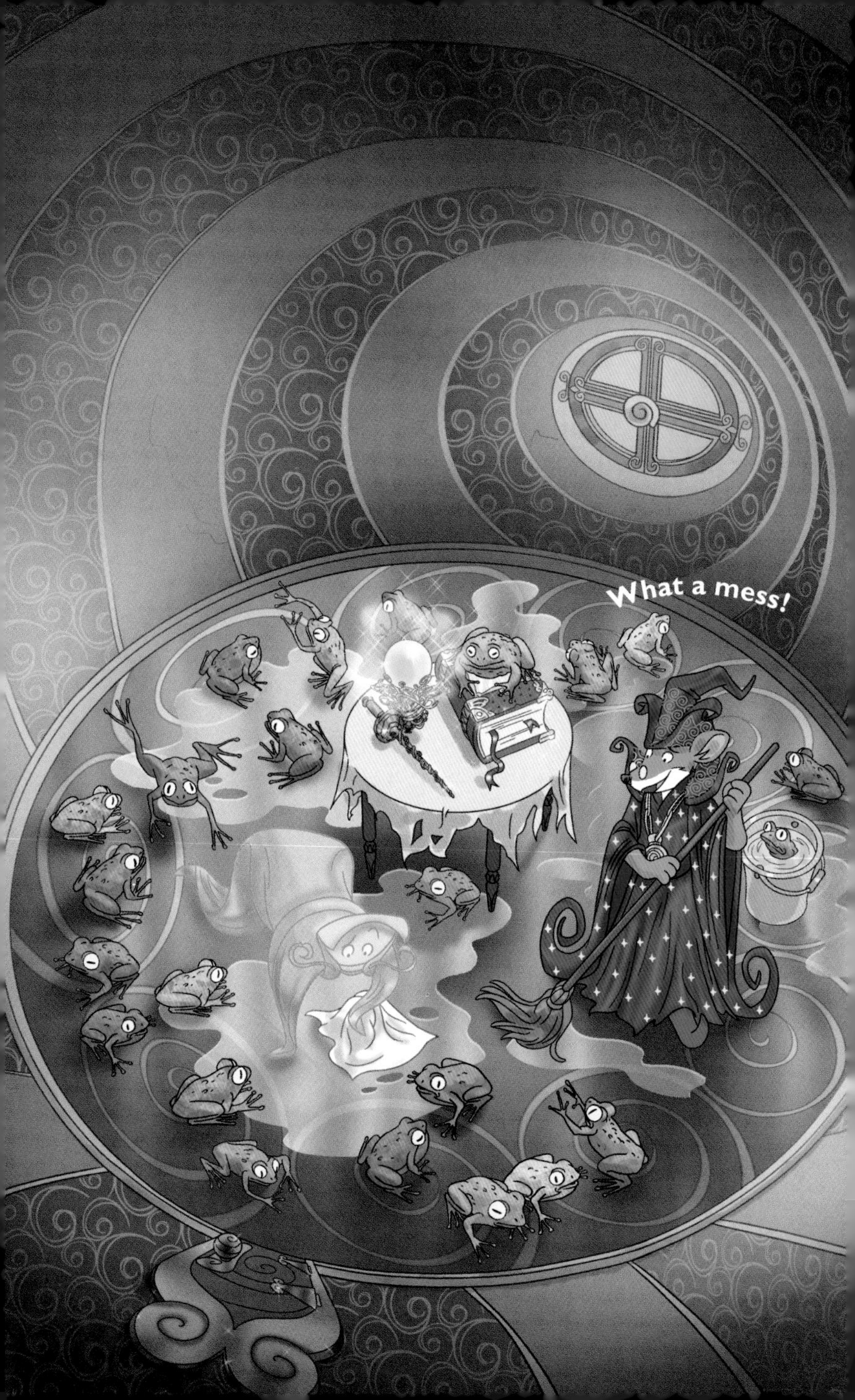
What a mess!

had used them to do a lot of damage! I realized just how **DANGEROUS** so much magic power could be. So instead of using another spell to clean up the room, I grabbed a MOP and a RAG. The Invisible Cloak came to my aid, mopping up water and wringing himself out in the sink.

What a good friend! He had tried to warn me that I was getting into trouble, but I hadn't listened.

"I'm so sorry!" I said. He forgave me right away. We hugged **HAPPILY** but then got serious.

I'm so sorry, my friend!

I forgive you!

How would we get rid of all those toads?

Luckily, the cloak had an **idea**. He pointed to a window, and I quickly opened it. The toads happily **LEAPED** right out the window, landing in the muddy moat below with a thousand joyful **SPLASHES**!

Ribbit!

Ribbit!

Ribbit!

Ribbit!

THE SHADOW PRISON

Once the floor was completely dry, I breathed a sigh of **RELIEF**. Then I removed the wizard clothes and put my **ARMOR** back on, which the cloak had brought for me. Finally, I put on the Invisible Cloak, took the THREE MAGICAL OBJECTS, and stepped out into the GLOOMY hallways of Shadow Tower in search of Queen Blossom.

I climbed UPSTAIRS and DOWNSTAIRS, I opened **LARGE** and small doors, I looked in ROOM after ROOM after ROOM after ROOM! But I didn't find a single **CLUE** to where Blossom might be.

I knew Blossom was imprisoned somewhere, and I had a feeling it was in that awful shadowy tower.

Discouraged, I sat down at the foot of a long,

twisting staircase. The Book of a Thousand Spells slipped from my paws and fell to the ground. It opened on a page that read: *The Most Powerful Magical Prisons in the Kingdom of Fantasy* . . .

The cloak pointed to the page excitedly. I read and reread the words slowly and looked at the drawing . . .

Magical prisons?

There are many magical prisons
in the Kingdom of Fantasy.
The most mysterious one is the
Shadow Prison! This is where
the wizard Longbeard hides
everything that he has made
vanish into thin air! Here's now
to find it:

Many have searched for the prison most feared —
The one that belongs to the wizard Longbeard!
Don't be fooled by his tricks and his lies,
This place can be found right in front of your eyes!
For all who are worthy and would like to know,
Do this one thing: blow, blow, blow!

Finally, I understood: *Blossom* was in the SHADOW PRISON! Did I just need to *blow* on the picture to open the door to the prison? Could it be that simple? Well, it was worth a try!

So I blew and blew and blew .

For a moment, it seemed like nothing was happening. Then the book began to vibrate, and the door in the drawing grew bigger and bigger and bigger. The door opened silently, and suddenly I was sucked through the open door by a magical force!

The Shadow Prison

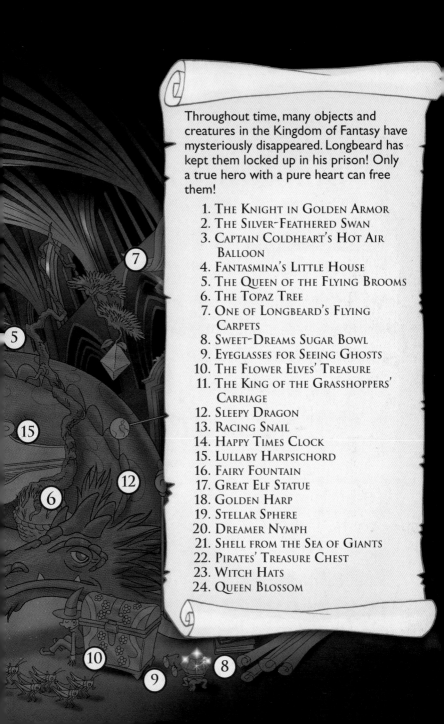

Throughout time, many objects and creatures in the Kingdom of Fantasy have mysteriously disappeared. Longbeard has kept them locked up in his prison! Only a true hero with a pure heart can free them!

1. THE KNIGHT IN GOLDEN ARMOR
2. THE SILVER-FEATHERED SWAN
3. CAPTAIN COLDHEART'S HOT AIR BALLOON
4. FANTASMINA'S LITTLE HOUSE
5. THE QUEEN OF THE FLYING BROOMS
6. THE TOPAZ TREE
7. ONE OF LONGBEARD'S FLYING CARPETS
8. SWEET-DREAMS SUGAR BOWL
9. EYEGLASSES FOR SEEING GHOSTS
10. THE FLOWER ELVES' TREASURE
11. THE KING OF THE GRASSHOPPERS' CARRIAGE
12. SLEEPY DRAGON
13. RACING SNAIL
14. HAPPY TIMES CLOCK
15. LULLABY HARPSICHORD
16. FAIRY FOUNTAIN
17. GREAT ELF STATUE
18. GOLDEN HARP
19. STELLAR SPHERE
20. DREAMER NYMPH
21. SHELL FROM THE SEA OF GIANTS
22. PIRATES' TREASURE CHEST
23. WITCH HATS
24. QUEEN BLOSSOM

ESCAPE FROM SHADOW PRISON!

The Shadow Prison contained many objects and fantastical creatures that LONGBEARD had been holding captive for a very LONG time. And there in the center of the room was Blossom, *Queen of the Fairies*!

I knelt down before her.

"Queen Blossom!" I exclaimed happily. "I finally found you!"

She smiled at me.

"I knew you would find me, Knight," she said sweetly. "I never doubted that you would discover the secret of the SHADOW PRISON!"

Suddenly, the Invisible Cloak began to pull **insistently** on my sleeve. He seemed very worried.

A moment later, I heard LONGBEARD SCREAMING.

"Wizard's Apprentice, how dare you disobey me?" he bellowed. "When I find you, I'll make you VANISH into thin air!"

Then I heard **Fluffy** meowing angrily.

"He's no Cat in Boots," Fluffy **growled**. "He's a wretched little rodent!"

Just before Longbeard and Fluffy burst into

Quick, let's go!

the Shadow Prison, I grabbed *Blossom's* hand and we dashed out the door, followed by all the fantastical creatures who had been **imprisoned** there with her. We all ran together toward the tower's exit.

"Quick, give me the magical items, Knight!" she ordered. "I need The Book of a Thousand Spells, the CRYSTAL SPHERE, and the WHiSPERiNG WAND."

The wand leaped **happily** into her hand. Then the sphere lit up with a thousand sparkles! And the book burst open to just the right page.

The spell at the top of the page read: *How to Crystallize a Shadow Castle and Transform Evil into Goodness!*

Blossom raised the Whispering Wand and recited the spell in a voice that sounded like a thousand nightingales singing:

"No more evil shall come to pass,
Once this Shadow Tower turns to glass!"

An instant later, the SHADOW TOWER transformed from a gloomy pillar of darkness into a castle made of clear crystal! Through the crystal walls, I saw Longbeard and Fussy De Whiskerpuss **WAVING** at us cheerfully. They had suddenly become good, too!

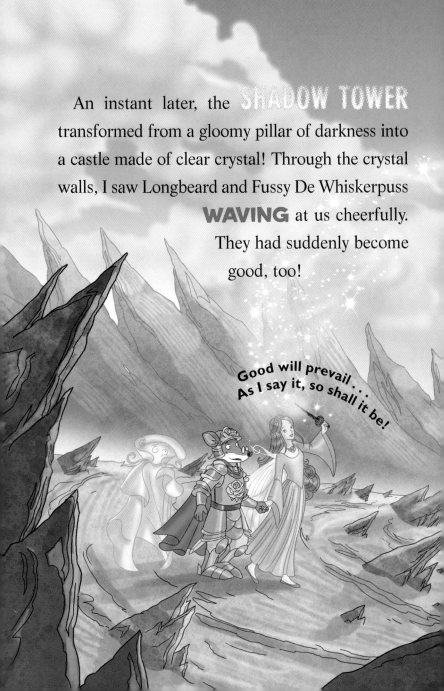

Good will prevail . . .
As I say it, so shall it be!

What an incredibly powerful spell!

I was feeling relaxed and happy when something came out of a bush to my right and caused me to nearly jump out of my fur.

"Cawww!" Cleverwing squawked. "That sure took you a while, Knight!"

But then he saw *Blossom* and his mood changed.

"Greetings, Queen!" he cawed politely. "I am Cleverwing, a noble raven."

He didn't have to say another **WORD** — Blossom seemed to already know his entire story. She handed him a **velvet** bag full of gold coins.

"Here is your payment, Cleverwing," she told him. "Even though you did it for the **wrong** reasons, you *did* help the knight complete his mission. But next time you might want to try helping someone in need without asking for anything in return!"

"I'll try, but I can't make any promises," Cleverwing replied as he flew off. "I'm afraid I **_adore_** scams too much! **CAWWW!**"

Blossom waved her wand and WHISPERED another spell:

"No longer will we have to roam, Whispering Wand, please take us home!"

Please take us home!

THE FAIRY SAFE

There was a flash of **blue** light. A moment later, we were in the Throne Room inside Crystal Castle! **HOW INCREDIBLE!**

"Ohhh!" the Invisible Cloak gasped **EXCITEDLY**. "What a marvelous place!"

Blossom reached out and gently touched one of the **CRYSTAL ROSES** that adorned the Throne Room walls. A panel moved immediately, revealing an enormouse **safe** behind it!

"This is the Fairy Safe," Blossom explained. "It is made of pure **FAIRY SILVER**, which is more **precious** than gold and **STRONGER** than steel."

She whispered a secret word under her breath and then stepped inside, motioning for me to follow her.

Fairy Safe

1. THE MAGIC WAND ROOM
2. THE ROOM OF CRYSTAL SPHERES
3. THE FAIRY JEWELS ROOM
4. THE FAIRY LIBRARY
5. THE LABYRINTH OF MIRRORS
6. THE FAIRY ARMOR AND WEAPONS ROOM
7. THE ROOM OF EVIL OBJECTS

It was so magnificent I could hardly believe my eyes!

Blossom led me to the center of the safe. I found myself standing before **SEVEN ROOMS** that were all petal shape. Each room was the home of a different type of magical **TREASURE**.

There were magic wands of all shapes and sizes, **TIMELESS WATCHES**, magic cauldrons, fairy jewels, enchanted mirrors, **talking books**, powerful rings, vials of fairy tears, crystal hearts, and a thousand other **magical objects**. Some of them were even **DARK** and **DANGEROUS** ones!

"Knight, the **most powerful** objects in the Kingdom of Fantasy are stored here," Blossom explained solemnly as she looked me right in the eye. "You have experimented with some of them yourself, so you know how **DANGEROUS** they can be! So from now on, I will keep The

Book of a Thousand Spells, the CRYSTAL SPHERE, and the WHISPERING WAND in this safe."

My fur turned **RED** with embarrassment as I remembered how the power of those objects nearly ruined me. I had gotten into so much trouble . . . and it could have been much, much **worse**!

But Blossom just smiled at me.

"Knight, I trust you!" she said. "That's why I will tell you the *secret word* that opens the safe. You will be the only one who knows it, because now you know your limits, and you recognize how **DANGEROUS** magic can be!"

Then she bent toward me . . . and whispered

the **secret word** in my ear.

"I will never tell a soul," I promised solemnly, placing my paw over my *heart*. "Your *secret* is safe with me, Queen Blossom!"

"I know!" she said, squeezing my paw *affectionately*. "Now, before I send you and the Invisible Cloak home, tell me what **rewards** I can offer you both, for saving me and the Kingdom of Fantasy?"

"Um, can I have some **special** beans that don't make me — uh — so **stinky**?" the cloak asked softly.

The queen snapped her fingers and a bag full of *golden beans* appeared. *they smelled like roses!*

The cloak giggled happily.

"Queen Blossom, I just did my duty," I replied. "I don't want **anything** in return."

"Thank you, brave and fearless Knight," Blossom replied, leaning over to *kiss* me gently on the top of my snout. "You will always be my hero!"

The next thing I knew, I was falling into a vortex of light . . .

THE RETURN TO NEW MOUSE CITY

RETURNING HOME!

The **gold light** was so strong I had to close my eyes. When I opened them again, I was in my **bed** in my house in New Mouse City.

A ray of gold light hit my snout. The sun was high in the sky and its rays were lighting up my bed! I looked at the clock. Cheese and crackers, it was already *nine in the morning*!

I looked around, bewildered. I still had the image of *Queen Blossom* in my head. What had just happened?

I sat down at my desk and turned on my computer to check my calendar. It was March 21! *Incredible!*

It seemed like so many days had gone by, but only one *magical* night had passed. I had traveled all the way to the *Kingdom of Fantasy* and

back again, even if it had been just a dream.

And I had learned a very **important** lesson on this journey. I knew now that there is no such thing as a **magic wand** that can fix everything in an **INSTANT**. Instead, honesty, sincerity, perseverance, dedication, and friendship are the tools that can do the most **GOOD** in life! And of those, the help of friends is most important!

I began to type immediately.

Tap, tap, tap!

Here's what I wrote:

My dear mouse friends, you know who I am, right?
  My name is Stilton, Geronimo Stilton, and I run *The Rodent's Gazette*, the most famouse newspaper on Mouse Island!
  I'm about to tell you the story of another one of my magical journeys to the Kingdom of Fantasy . . .

I stopped and **SQUEAKED** in satisfaction.

"This isn't a bad beginning at all . . ." I said aloud.

I continued to write all day, and the next day, and the next day, for **days**, weeks, and months . . .

I gave it my all and asked for **HELP** from

Dear mouse friends . . .

my friends when I needed it. After many months, the book was finally **READY**! I invited all my family and friends to **CELEBRATE** and **SHARE** my happiness with me.

Dear readers, I wish you could have been there, too! If you had been, I would have given you each a big **hug**, and I would have told you that the **real magic** in life is . . .

FANTASIAN ALPHABET

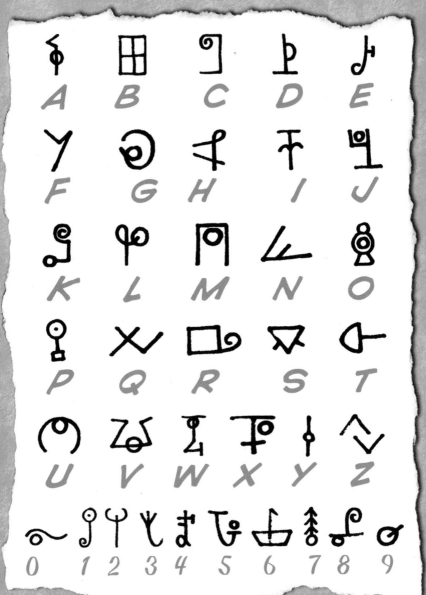

SOLUTIONS

Page 46

Page 100–101
There are 28 invisible spiders.

Page 158–159
There are 20 candles.

Page 240–241

Page 270–271
There are 105 toads.

ABOUT THE AUTHOR

 Born in New Mouse City, Mouse Island, **GERONIMO STILTON** is Rattus Emeritus of Mousomorphic Literature and of Neo-Ratonic Comparative Philosophy. For the past twenty years, he has been running *The Rodent's Gazette*, New Mouse City's most widely read daily newspaper.

Stilton was awarded the Ratitzer Prize for his scoops on *The Curse of the Cheese Pyramid* and *The Search for Sunken Treasure*. He has also received the Andersen 2000 Prize for Personality of the Year. One of his bestsellers won the 2002 eBook Award for world's best ratlings' electronic book. His works have been published all over the globe.

In his spare time, Mr. Stilton collects antique cheese rinds and plays golf. But what he most enjoys is telling stories to his nephew Benjamin.

Don't miss any of my adventures in the Kingdom of Fantasy!

THE KINGDOM OF FANTASY

THE QUEST FOR PARADISE:
THE RETURN TO THE KINGDOM OF FANTASY

THE AMAZING VOYAGE:
THE THIRD ADVENTURE IN THE KINGDOM OF FANTASY

THE DRAGON PROPHECY:
THE FOURTH ADVENTURE IN THE KINGDOM OF FANTASY

THE VOLCANO OF FIRE:
THE FIFTH ADVENTURE IN THE KINGDOM OF FANTASY

THE SEARCH FOR TREASURE:
THE SIXTH ADVENTURE IN THE KINGDOM OF FANTASY

THE ENCHANTED CHARMS:
THE SEVENTH ADVENTURE IN THE KINGDOM OF FANTASY

THE PHOENIX OF DESTINY:
AN EPIC KINGDOM OF FANTASY ADVENTURE

THE HOUR OF MAGIC:
THE EIGHTH ADVENTURE IN THE KINGDOM OF FANTASY

THE WIZARD'S WAND:
THE NINTH ADVENTURE IN THE KINGDOM OF FANTASY

Be sure to read all my fabumouse adventures!

 **#1 Lost Treasure of the Emerald Eye**

 **#2 The Curse of the Cheese Pyramid**

 **#3 Cat and Mouse in a Haunted House**

 **#4 I'm Too Fond of My Fur!**

 **#5 Four Mice Deep in the Jungle**

 **#6 Paws Off, Cheddarface!**

 **#7 Red Pizzas for a Blue Count**

 **#8 Attack of the Bandit Cats**

 **#9 A Fabumouse Vacation for Geronimo**

 **#10 All Because of a Cup of Coffee**

 **#11 It's Halloween, You 'Fraidy Mouse!**

 **#12 Merry Christmas, Geronimo!**

 **#13 The Phantom of the Subway**

 **#14 The Temple of the Ruby of Fire**

 **#15 The Mona Mousa Code**

 **#16 A Cheese-Colored Camper**

 **#17 Watch Your Whiskers, Stilton!**

 **#18 Shipwreck on the Pirate Islands**

 **#19 My Name Is Stilton, Geronimo Stilton**

 **#20 Surf's Up, Geronimo!**

#21 The Wild, Wild West   **#22 The Secret of Cacklefur Castle**   **A Christmas Tale**   **#23 Valentine's Day Disaster**   **#24 Field Trip to Niagara Falls**

#25 The Search for Sunken Treasure   **#26 The Mummy with No Name**   **#27 The Christmas Toy Factory**   **#28 Wedding Crasher**   **#29 Down and Out Down Under**

#30 The Mouse Island Marathon   **#31 The Mysterious Cheese Thief**   **Christmas Catastrophe**   **#32 Valley of the Giant Skeletons**   **#33 Geronimo and the Gold Medal Mystery**

#34 Geronimo Stilton, Secret Agent   **#35 A Very Merry Christmas**   **#36 Geronimo's Valentine**   **#37 The Race Across America**   **#38 A Fabumouse School Adventure**

#39 Singing Sensation   **#40 The Karate Mouse**   **#41 Mighty Mount Kilimanjaro**   **#42 The Peculiar Pumpkin Thief**   **#43 I'm Not a Supermouse!**

#44 The Giant Diamond Robbery

#45 Save the White Whale!

#46 The Haunted Castle

#47 Run for the Hills, Geronimo!

#48 The Mystery in Venice

#49 The Way of the Samurai

#50 This Hotel Is Haunted!

#51 The Enormouse Pearl Heist

#52 Mouse in Space!

#53 Rumble in the Jungle

#54 Get into Gear, Stilton!

#55 The Golden Statue Plot

#56 Flight of the Red Bandit

The Hunt for the Golden Book

#57 The Stinky Cheese Vacation

#58 The Super Chef Contest

#59 Welcome to Moldy Manor

The Hunt for the Curious Cheese

#60 The Treasure of Easter Island

#61 Mouse House Hunter

#62 Mouse Overboard!

The Hunt for the Secret Papyrus

#63 The Cheese Experiment

#64 Magical Mission